How I got
RICH
writing
$$C
PAPERS

How I got RICH writing $$C PAPERS

Andy Hueller

Sweetwater Books
An Imprint of Cedar Fort, Inc.
Springville, Utah

ISBN 13: 978-1-4621-1058-2

Published by Sweetwater Books, an imprint of Cedar Fort, Inc., 2373 W. 700 S., Springville, UT 84663
Distributed by Cedar Fort, Inc., www.cedarfort.com

LIBRARY OF CONGRESS CATALOGING-IN-PUBLICATION DATA

Hueller, Andy, author.
 How I got rich writing C papers / Andy Hueller.
    pages cm
 Summary: Charles makes money by writing essays for his high school classmates, and as he outlines his method, he teaches the reader how to write his or her own essays.
 Includes bibliographical references and index.
 ISBN 978-1-4621-1058-2 (alk. paper)
 1. Fiction. gsafd [1. Schools--Fiction. 2. Writing--Fiction.] I. Title.
 PZ7.H8694How 2012
 [Fic]--dc23
                              2012041534

Illustrations by Daniela Tiedemann
Cover design by Angela D. Olsen
Cover design © 2013 by Lyle Mortimer
Typeset and edited by Melissa J. Caldwell

Printed in the United States of America

10 9 8 7 6 5 4 3 2 1

To my other brother, Marc.

If patience involves lots of whining,
no one has more of it.
But you do it so well.

Other books by
Andy Hueller

Dizzy Fantastic and Her Flying Bicycle
Skipping Stones at the Center of the Earth

Monday, March 1

Today begins with a text message. It will end, I presume, with at least one Nerf dart reaching its target.

A minute before my alarm is set to wake me, my cell phone bellows the Jaws music that means someone has texted me. I roll over and open my phone. The text, from Chris Rinkles, looks like this:

> We r taking blu bk test in English.
> Got plan?!?!?!?

I sigh. I've been waiting for this—for one of my customers to hear about the Blue Book exam from a teacher and register that it may be a problem, given that he hasn't written his own essay in four years. I wrote my response to questions like Chris's weeks ago and saved it as a draft. I send it to him now:

> I'm working on it. Don't worry.

I probably should have included the word *yet*, as in "Don't worry yet." Because he's not going to like my plan.

My Parting Gift

I'll finish my senior year of high school in a few long months, and I guess I'm getting sentimental or big-hearted. Or something. I read recently that when S. E. Hinton's *The Outsiders* was first published, it was banned by a lot of libraries. Too much violence perhaps. Supposedly, teenagers all over purchased copies and passed them around in secret. It was a story that spoke to them, and they needed to read it. That sounds pretty impressive to me, and gets me thinking maybe you all are capable of sharing what I've learned without getting adults involved. Maybe. Plus, there's the whole Blue Book ordeal coming up, and I'm putting a lot of faith in my peers, which means there's a good chance I'll get caught. If I'm going to have an opportunity to write down what I know and prepare it for dissemination, this is it.

This all started as a way to make money—lots and lots of money. But soon, assuming I don't get caught and then expelled, I'll be off to college, and it would be a shame to not pass on what I've learned these past four years. We all want to leave a legacy, right? If everything goes to plan, my legacy will feature two accomplishments:

1. Writing essays for my classmates while I make money and none of us gets caught.
2. Winning the Nerf War→ our senior year.

I guess my legacy's in your hands now. Well, literally. You are literally holding in your hands my account of how I got rich writing essays and achieved immortality (if all goes to plan) through this year's Nerf War, the annual everybody-for-himself competition among seniors at my high school.

Good luck.

Just leave me out of it from here on. I'm doing my good deed for the year, and I'm tired. Of course, if you can find a way to contact me and show your gratitude with a generous financial donation, I'm all ears.

CRD•

→ Why do I care about winning the Nerf War, I, the soon-to-be college student who already has established a flourishing business? I'm not quite sure, but I do. So you know: Senior-year Nerf War has four guidelines, created by some senior class in some other school in some other decade: 1. You begin with an index card with another senior's name on it. 2. You hunt down that person (outside of school and on foot—that means no drive-bys), shoot her with a Nerf dart, and take her index card. 3. You go after the person whose name is on that card next. 4. Remember: Someone always has your name on an index card as well.

• Two things: 1. These aren't my initials. As an additional

Still Monday, March 1

Near the end of first-period English class, Mrs. Hillberry hands back essays she graded. The one with my name has a B written on the top of the front page. *Mrs. Hillberry, you got it right,* I think. The paper deserves a B. I survey the room. Lisa Kent—the ever-beautiful Lisa Kent with the big brown eyes—has an essay with an A on it, of course. Bill Thompson's has a B-minus, too high a grade. Sidney Little's grade isn't on the front. Mrs. Hillberry obviously didn't want to expose Sidney to any embarrassment a low grade might cause her. I watch Sidney flip to the back of her essay,

---

precaution—one more line of defense so nobody hunts me down at college with flashlights and sirens and dogs—I don't use my actual name in this document. Instead I call myself Charles Remington Dremmel. I think it sounds cool. 2. I use footnotes a lot. You can ignore them if you want. Heck, you can do anything you want. You don't need to read this book at all. I do put valuable information in the footnotes, though. Oh, and 3. I use symbols instead of numbers for my footnotes because I like the look of them better. Deal with it, MLA (Modern Language Association).

where she finds her D-plus. Good. I smile to myself. Hey—it's what she paid for.

I tell Sid just this when she approaches me after class. "And I don't talk business inside this building, either," I add. I look over both my shoulders. I admit, it's not just business that has me on edge. I'm a bit anxious all the time these days, expecting someone to step out from behind a locker and shoot me in the face with a foam dart. It's against the rules to carry out a hit in school, but it's happened in past years and has led to controversial decisions about whether or not passing time counts as "in school."

"I know, I know. I was coming to say thank you. As long as I pass this class, I'll graduate with my friends." Sid L. is my newest customer.

"Well, if you ever want something more," I whisper, "you know, a higher grade, maybe think about skipping a day or two of school to pick up extra shifts at Terry's." She's been ringing up groceries since last summer. "I know we're running out of time, but you still have three essays to turn in. You could earn a couple C-pluses and finish the year with a B essay. Bs aren't cheap, but they make grandparents happy."

"Yeah. Maybe. Let me think about it."

It's the wise response. As I told Sid, Bs aren't cheap.

I'm a senior, and I've been writing my classmates' papers for four years. The idea came to me as a seventh grader, actually, when my friend Doug was swamped with schoolwork, baseball, and his bar mitzvah, and he didn't turn in his paper on time. His teacher said she was writing an email home if he didn't get the paper in the next day.

"I can write you a passing paper in a few minutes," I told him back then. It actually took twenty-seven minutes that first time, despite it being a short paper for middle school and not nearly as sophisticated as many of the essays I've written for him and others since. I was only in seventh grade, and I hadn't yet hit my stride. As we rejoiced in his B-minus two weeks later, a business idea was born. I spent eighth grade polishing my strategy. My business wouldn't take off, I knew, until ninth grade.

Ninth grade. That's when we all moved from the middle school to the high school. We not only moved to a new building; we moved to increased expectations from teachers and parents. In a couple years, college searches would clutter our schedules. Can't-miss weekend parties at the homes of out-of-town parents would presume priority. Some of us found jobs—and with them, new disposable incomes! Even as an eighth grader, I had known this would all add up to one thing: a flourishing business. Track practice and a social life could wait for me. I was going to be rich.

My Whatever-you-want-to-call-it

My formula for success, my business model, my way of doing things, my whatever-you-want-to-call-it—it's simple.

1. Set-in-stone prices.

$5 .... D
$10 C
$20 ....B
$100 .... A

I always shoot for pluses—D-plus, C-plus, B-plus—to allow for teacher error. A customer's happy if she gets a higher grade; she's ticked off if she gets a lower grade. So I play it conservatively. Often, I feel like a philanthropist, to tell you the truth, like I'm working pro bono, as my classmates pay for Cs and teachers let them off the hook with B-minuses. Okay, so they're not lowering or destroying writing standards the way some adults say they are, but they *are* hurting my profit margin.

2. Binding contracts
and careful, deliberate progress.

When my offer made its hush-hush way around to students in my ninth-grade class (ninety-eight of them in all)—my offer, that is, to forever remove paper writing from their busy high school lives—I sat down with each interested customer (thirty-three of them), one on one. I still do this with each new customer. Together, we read fastidiously the contract I drafted.

Writing Services Contract

In concordance with the conversation between Mr. Charles Remington Dremmel (service provider) and

_____ (customer), Mr. Dremmel will compose, proof, and print every written assignment for the _____ school year. Per the customer's decision, each of these papers will earn this grade (circle **one**):

$5.............D
$10...........C
$20...........B
$100.........A

Any and all grade upswings will be gradual and deliberate, so as not to attract suspicion toward technically unethical contracted business agreements.

The customer will be responsible for making the corresponding payment **at least four days** prior to the assignment's due date. Late payment will result in the assignment's late submission.

The paper will be handed to the customer as many days late as is his/her payment. Any lowered grade from the teacher due to lateness will be the customer's responsibility. The customer must follow any other timetable requirements presented by the service provider.

This is a legal and binding contract.

Signed,

Charles Remington Dremmel   _____

Charles Remington Dremmel,   (Customer)
Service Provider

After reviewing the contract with a client, I always reinforce what it says: There will be no jumping from Ds or even Cs to As. Obviously too suspicious. And once the contract gets signed, I explain, there will be no looking back. That's right. The signee can never turn in her* own English or history paper+ that school year. Not even a typed journal entry or response paragraph. When a teacher assigns small in-class writings, there's nothing to worry about. Teachers don't expect these to be polished pieces. Many don't read them as carefully, either. (How misguided is that, by the way? A small in-class piece is a perfectly authentic sample of a student's writing, untouched by parents, tutors, or other students, and waiting to be read. That's precisely what a teacher *should* read closely, if you ask me.) We're not taking any chances on typed take-home assignments, however. I don't want a teacher mumbling to herself, "Why is she comma splicing all of a sudden?"

---

* You'll notice that I interchange the gendered pronouns: *he*, *she*, *his*, *her*. We all use *they* and *their* in conversation because we don't, in these days of equal opportunity, feel comfortable with male pronouns representing both men and women. But English teachers pedantically point out that *they* is a plural pronoun. I could keep repeating the phrases *he or she* and *his or her* (or the loathsome *he/she* and *his/her*), but English teachers are awfully impressed when a writer can interchange *he* and *she*, *his* and *her*. That way, you use a singular pronoun (check!), you don't give either gender dominance over the other (check!), you demonstrate concision (check!), and you avoid repetition (check!). I do this—interchange gendered pronouns—for students who pay for A papers, and I do it for my friend Doug and the lovely Lisa Kent. In eighth grade, Lisa wrote in my yearbook, "You make me laugh. I hope we have a class together next year." I'm not an idiot, and I know she may have written this in pretty much everybody's yearbook, but I can't help it. Those brown eyes. I just keep on writing free A essays for her semester after semester.

+ I don't write math, science, or foreign language papers. Those aren't read in the same way, they require skills I don't have, and English teachers don't talk to those other teachers about student writing, anyway.

Oh, you should know: The comma splice is my pet peeve. No, it's more than that. It's my nightmare. Nothing this side of genocide annoys me more. My eighth-grade English teacher, Mr. Klerman, showed us all how to avoid them, and it drives me insane that so many people around me (including my parents and some of my teachers) still put a wimpy, scrawny comma between two independent clauses.[?] That's expecting the comma to support too much weight. It's like asking a wide receiver to pancake block two 300-pound defensive tackles coming from different directions at the same time. More on comma splices later.

3. A payment plan I believe in.

None of this "I'm probably selling my PS3" crap. Seriously: Get a job, or we're not having this conversation.

4. All business must be conducted at my house—not at school!

[?] What's an *independent clause*? A fair question. It's a very technical-sounding term that means this: words put together so they could stand on their own as a complete sentence. So "The dog upchucked" is an independent clause. It has a something (a dog) doing something (in this case, upchucking). "The dog" all on its own is not a complete sentence, because it only has a something and doesn't say what that something is doing. Likewise, "upchucking" on its own is not an independent clause, because it's something one does, but a reader doesn't know who did it. Got it? Lots of great sentences aren't complete sentences, of course, but a complete sentence does have a subject and a predicate, a something doing something, and a comma can't sit on its own between two complete sentences.

My customers swing by my house before school the day the assignment's due. I live three blocks from school, in a small bungalow house my parents have been renting from my grandmother pretty much since they got married, so I'm on everybody's way, and I don't want any adult seeing essays change hands at school. A customer doesn't leave my porch, however, until she's read the essay I wrote for her. This avoids blank stares and stuttering when teachers ask clarifying questions in or after class.

And finally, most importantly . . .

5. Thought Farts.

Each of my customers must keep a notebook with him for an hour each day. On Mondays, Wednesdays, and Fridays, it should be out during a class of the customer's choosing. I don't need to worry about someone getting caught because, hey, they're just taking notes, which is what they should be doing, right? On Tuesday and Thursday, the notebook needs to be out during transit between home and school, school and home, or at some extracurricular activity. On the weekend, the Thought Farts must be recorded at home when near family. All I ask is that a customer writes down his thoughts and turns these thoughts in to me for review each week. If I'm going to pretend to be him, I need to understand how he thinks and what he thinks about.

Let me give you an example of why this is important. Heading into our junior year baseline essays (which teachers use to assess where each student is, as a writer, at the beginning of the school year), the teachers apparently caved. They tried to relate to us, which is always dangerous. Four superhero movies had hit theaters that summer, and statistics showed that a lot of teenagers went and saw them. So the English teachers asked us to write a response essay to this question: If you could have any superpower, which would you choose and why?

Maybe you're thinking that doesn't sound so hard. Try writing sixty-seven of them. (Thirty-four new students had signed up after ninth grade—nine before sophomore year, twenty-five before junior year, when they began visiting colleges and needed to think about writing essays for those colleges.) I needed to bring enough variety of superpowers, experiences, and writing styles to the collection that English teachers would believe sixty-seven different students wrote them. One thing I had going for me: I knew every teacher would assume that half the class wouldn't think very hard and would say they wanted to *fly* more than anything—I bet if you go ask your friends right now, you'll get the same unimaginative results—which made my job a little easier. Still, it's not easy writing the same assignment for so many people. Once the school year begins, we're all separated into different classrooms and our teachers give us slightly different assignments due on slightly different dates, which makes my job a lot more manageable. With the first assignment of the year, English teachers get together and decide what they're going to make students write about. They probably even believe students will look forward to writing the assignment, because they come up with something cutesy like this superpowers assignment. Two years ago, the first assignment asked us to describe the ideal school in a two-page essay. (In the A paper I wrote for Lisa Kent,♥ I admitted that at the ideal school students wouldn't go to school every day. They would go on field trips all over, and they would get to make choices each morning about how they would spend their day. There would be

---

♥ In eighth-grade social studies, Lisa sat in the desk behind me. She wore these Birkenstock clogs in a couple different colors, and she rested them on the tray at the bottom of my desk. Sometimes she'd touch me on the shoulder to ask me questions about whatever we were doing in class. She was Jasmine in the middle-school play *Aladdin* that year, and I still want to go on a magic carpet ride with her. That probably meant something more innocent in eighth grade than it does now. Anyway, she was (is) this popular girl and still she kissed Benjamin Tullie, this dorky kid who was the only boy Ms. Trents, the drama teacher, could find to play the lead in the play. Sitting in the audience I wished more than anything that I could trade lives with Benjamin Tullie. It was enough to want to beat him up, if I hadn't also been a scrawny dork. So I fell in love with Lisa that year and never stopped loving her. I didn't need her for my business, but I think she deserves to have A papers written for her—like Daisy Buchannan deserves to have Jay Gatsby build her a house. And as far as I know, Lisa has never run over anyone with a car, which is a good thing. If you don't know what I'm talking about, read F. Scott Fitzgerald's *The Great Gatsby*. Or if you don't want to read a book, maybe you can consider her Princess Peach from *Super Mario Bros.* I just can't help but save her from writing her own papers, even when I risk my business by doing it for free. Saving her—or writing essays for her—is part of who I am. Of course, she and I haven't talked since eighth grade, perhaps because I avoid her at all costs, even asking Doug to give her her essays, because I know I'll say something stupid.

no homework assigned by some adult because the adult feels it's good for you. You can get away with this kind of honesty in an A paper, because if you devote enough time to the truth, nothing's more compelling.) Anyway, it was the first writing assignment of junior year that convinced me to require Thought Farts from my customers. I did come up with some clever superpowers, too; they fit the customers I gave them to, even if they never would have come up with them on their own.

Take Bryant Washington. He needed his mom to believe he'd paid attention in summer school and had learned to write a mostly coherent essay. (Scenarios like this lead to money in my pocket.) He handed me these Thought Farts:

At Home
* Parents arguing about something.
* I don't want to do homework or take these notes, I want to sleep.
* My sisters need to tern off that stupid TV with there stupid animals show.
* Hey thats the ice creme truck bell. i used to like the ice creme truck. Wait why do you need to know that? This is stupid, your stupid.
* im not doing any more of these notes, ill just write my own paper and save the money.

He changed his mind by the time he handed his Thought Farts over to me, and without his Thought Farts, I couldn't have come up with this gem:

Superpowers Essay

Before I tell you what superhero identity I'd choose if I could have any, please believe me that I'm no sissy. I don't usually go for fairy tales, and I mean I'm pretty tough if you ask me. I can put up with a lot. Maybe that's why I don't need to fly or run really really fast. I don't need to escape my problems or anything. I just need to be able to ignore them sometimes. I don't want any superhuman abilities to help me get through the day. I just want a good night's sleep. That's why I choose Sleeping Beauty. Yeah, that's right, Sleeping Beauty. You got a problem with that? For my superpower, I want the ability to sleep through anything for eight hours.

I want to sleep through my parents' arguing and the TV they turn on loud to try to block out their arguing. (It doesn't work.) I want to sleep through my little sisters' crying about my parents' fighting and from hunger and whatever else. I want to sleep through the ambulance and police sirens outside my window, where the dealers deal and the homeless suffer.

Hey—this is my life, and I don't want someone else's. I'm just saying, I want to wake up and live my life and fix the lives of my family and neighbors on a full night's sleep. So, yeah: Call me Sleeping Beauty. I hope you do.

Honestly, I shot myself in the foot with this essay. All the kid asked for was a C (it's all he could afford), and here he gets a B-plus. All because I didn't take the sympathy vote into account. Yeah, the essay's only three paragraphs long, and it never develops even one example, but teachers are suckers for the heartfelt and pitiful. More than that, they're suckers for *voice*. I gave Bryant attitude, and he expresses himself here (or I express a fake him here) clearly if not deeply. I just had to pull together several different Thought Farts to make Bryant's home life much more dramatic than it really is. I also made the mistake of punctuating and spelling helpfully⊕ here. Believe me—no C-plus essay

---

⊕ I say punctuate and spell *helpfully* and not *correctly* because while we have rules regarding punctuation and spelling, these rules have adapted over time. The point isn't ever to follow rules—it's to help your reader understand your point. We use punctuation to show readers where the parts of our sentences are, just like we've agreed on how to spell most words so readers can rely on them being spelled a certain way. Go read something written hundreds of years ago—say, the Constitution of the United States. You'll see words spelled differently, and *wow!* did our Founding Fathers love their capital letters!

I've written since has been so polished. I've been stuck writing B papers for Bryant (while he only pays for Cs!) ever since. And yes, my customers often write spiteful stuff directed at me in their notes. You know what, though? Bryant, just like all the rest of them, keeps paying me. Once you begin your own essay-writing business, you'll hear criticism from your customers, too. But so what? You can take a few insults from someone who's helping you with your college tuition, right?

Anyway, clients do more of the work than they know while they write down their Thought Farts. Mr. Klerman told our class, "Writing is thinking." Sounds like feces-infested teacher advice, I know, but it's true. Classmates' notes always jump-start my writing for them, and I don't really know what connections I'll make in their papers until I start writing.

6. A Room of One's Own

That's the title of an essay you might have to read in high school or college. It's also an essential concept if you want to run a business. The house my family rents is small, with no basement, and I used to sleep on the family room couch. When I started my business, I convinced my parents to let me move upstairs into the attic—not by telling them about my business, mind you. I spent a couple days wiping down the place so there weren't many spiders or cobwebs left. It gets really hot in the summer and really cold in the winter, but at least I can get away from my parents when they're home. To write as many essays as quickly as I do, I need my own space. When my parents aren't home, I write on the dining-room table instead.

7. A Dog

We have an Airedale named Banjo. Sometimes an entrepreneur needs to think for himself. When he does, there's no better way to get alone with his thoughts than a walk with the dog.

And there you have it: my business plan or whatever you want to call it.

✳ ✳ ✳ ✳ ✳

Monday's final bell sounds. I slide past my class-mates and out of my eighth-period science lab. I get to the middle of the hall and hold a line, between two streams of traffic, as if on a rail. I walk fast enough that I'm almost jogging. I need to get to my locker as soon as possible. Why does my eighth-period class need to be on the other side of the school from my locker?

When I get to my locker, I kick the bottom and the door swings open. I push my science and math books to the back of the top shelf, snatch my backpack (already packed with the novels my customers are reading in English, my laptop, and my Quick 16 Blaster), and turn to run down the hallway, elbowing my locker closed as I move on.

Two locker bays away, I see Lisa Kent at her locker.

She's loading her books into her bag, her brown eyes closed as she listens to music, it appears, streaming from her iPod. I want to stop, ask her what she's listening to, and offer to help her carry her books (That's what a guy's supposed to do, right, if he wants to do more than hold her books the next time?), but I know I don't have time and can't muster the confidence, anyway. As I said, she and I haven't really spoken since eighth grade. Passing by her locker, I can't help but glance, and I swear for a moment that our eyes meet in the mirror she has magnetized to the inside of her locker door. I know, of course, deep down, that she's just looking at her makeup or hair. So instead I race by her to the doors at the end of the hall. Pushing them open, I break into a dead sprint to the copse of trees on the eastern border of campus. There's a path that winds through this copse, allowing students to avoid walking around four blocks of houses. I stay away from this path now, stomping instead through damp leaves until I get to a tree—an oak—with low branches that make it easy to climb.

I clamber up the tree and get settled on a branch fifteen feet from the ground, directly over the path. I pull from my backpack my yellow Quick 16 Blaster, already loaded, take a deep breath, wipe sweat from my brow and face with my shirtsleeve, and wait. I take the index card that says HENRY WILSON from my pocket.

"So, Henry Wilson, this is it," I say. "Any last words?" And then I want to slap myself in the face. Really? That's the best I could come up with?

I'm still remonstrating myself when I hear footsteps on the path just outside of sight. I know it's him because I followed him down the path last week, even as I looked over my shoulders every second to make sure no one was watching me.

And then, there he is. It's hard to miss Henry's big mess of curly brown clown's hair. He's tall and slight, a cross-country runner. As usual, Henry is walking with his younger sister, Henrietta (yep—their parents did that to them), who's in ninth grade. She's a cross-country runner too.

"Patience," I tell myself. "Patience." I know I need to wait until Henry is directly below me to make sure this won't fail. I know, also, that I don't need to rush. I have all day.

And that's when four darts whizz by my ear.

"What the—" I say, and, acting on instincts, scramble down the tree, keeping the trunk between me and where the darts came from. I want to figure out who sent it my way, but there's no way to do this without exposing myself. Six more darts miss me, three on each side of the trunk. A voice shouts, "You hit, Dremmel?" Whose voice is it? My heart's pumping, I'm not hearing clearly, and all that registers is that it's deep, a guy's— but I wasn't listening closely enough, and it could be any guy in the senior class. I don't need to answer, because I'm not hit, but I know I can't stay where I am. By this time, Henry and Henrietta have turned to sprint the other way, back to where they came from, and I need to make a decision fast. I might be able to catch them if I run after them. They're only thirty feet from me, but then again they're faster than I am and certainly have more endurance. Plus, will my own stalker assume I'll chase after them?

I go the other way, instead, allowing the winding path to weave me in and out of trees and their branches. There are no leaves on the trees now, but the branches, I hope, will be enough to block any darts. I'm not sure if any others are fired, but when I leave the copse I haven't been hit.

I can't give up on Henry. Now that he knows I'm after him, he'll be an awfully difficult target in the days to come. I better catch up with him before he has the chance to strategize, find new routes home, or revise his schedule. I'm not sure of their address. I probably should have looked it up in a phone book, but I thought I had Henry dead to rights. I do, however, know my way around the neighborhood. I live here, too. I run between two houses to the sidewalk in front of them. I already have a stitch in my side, and I make a promise to myself that in college, when I no longer run an essay-writing business, I'll work out more regularly. Do intramurals or something.

I run up the sidewalk to the corner of the block, breathing hard, still carrying my backpack, my Nerf gun in my right hand. At the corner, I barely slow down to turn right and keep sprinting. Halfway down the block, I catch a break. Henry and Henrietta, looking behind them, appear from around the corner. When they turn and see me, Henry has a garage door opener in his hand, and he points it in front of him and to his left. The door to the nearest house's garage is already open, and now it begins to close. They never break stride as they gallop off the sidewalk and run through the front lawn. They're gazelles to my portly lion. We reach the driveway at the same time, but they're at the top of it, slinging their backpacks under the closing door and then ducking under it themselves. I pull the trigger and pump out eight shots as the door closes behind them. I hope I've hit Henry's legs under the closing door.

"Did I get you, Henry?" I yell.

Nobody responds.

Then the door begins to climb and groan open. Henry steps out as his sister says, "Whoa. That was intense."

Henry's nodding. He doesn't look winded at all. "Yeah—you got me, Charles." He says it with disappointment in his voice, but he's grinning. "Nice shots."

After he's handed me his index card, we shake hands, and I walk home, tired and sweaty. The index card says MARC PRIDE.

Now I need to figure out who's after me.

Tuesday, March 2

I wake up exhausted. By rule, I don't turn my cell phone off at night as a courtesy to my clients. Sometimes a client needs to reach me because she had a conversation with a teacher who told her to make sure to include something in her paper, or her parents told her that evening that she needs to drive a younger brother to school in the morning and so she can't make it to my house to pick up her paper, or she's sick,[+] or whatever. In such cases, I need to take the call or read the text. Last night, though, my phone rang and rang; Jaws music played behind my dreams. Every time I turned a corner, I expected someone or something (a man-eating landshark like in those old Saturday Night Live sketches?[^]) to waylay me. I guess my two missions—writing and Nerf—have now gotten tangled in my

---

+ I never, ever, ever allow sick people near me. If they get me sick, I don't have the energy to do my job.

^ YouTube it.

subconscious. And in my reality, too. There was my hot pursuit of Henry Wilson yesterday, even as I too was pursued; plus, every time I turned a corner at school, someone wanted to ask me about the upcoming Blue Book exam, which of course breaks my "No business at school" rule. Unfortunately, now there's no avoiding it. The news about the Blue Book exam in a few months has spread like the flu. It terrifies my classmates to think that they'll need to write an entire essay in class on their own, and that this will be an assignment their teachers read carefully. The idea scares me, too. I don't want to be caught. How, my classmates wonder, can Charles write in-class essays for us? Last night I replied to every client with the same text:

I'm working on it. Don't worry.

Max Latterly, class jerk, replied,

u better b

I'm not intimidated by Max, even though he is a big guy who plays hockey, but I do understand his fear. I hate when something feels out of my control, too. I wrote earlier that, if classmates knew my plan, they would worry. Well, I'm the one who really needs to worry. I know I'll work out all the details, but will my classmates come through for themselves and for me? I won't spring my plan on them until it's too late for them to argue.

Groggily, I get out of bed and head for the shower.

In the shower, I replay that voice—"You hit, Dremmel?" again and again. It's no good. It's not mine, it's not Henry Wilson's, and it's not Marc Pride's. It's not a girl's voice. After that, I have no idea.

✳ ✳ ✳ ✳ ✳

A Formula: D, C, and B Papers

So you want to know how I can reliably produce D, C, B, and A papers? Like my business model, my writing formula is simple. There's a formula English teachers use to grade papers, whether they acknowledge the formula or not. Most *do* acknowledge it, by the way; students just don't listen. Most teachers hand out lists of expectations; some even hand out the very rubrics they'll use to assess the papers; and still students don't take the time to make sure everything on the list or rubric is also in their essay. (If any teacher ends up reading this somehow, hear me roar: Simply handing out a list of expectations doesn't help anyone. Do *you* read whatever they hand you in faculty meetings? You might want to sit down with your students and break down what a good essay looks like—you know, like I'm doing here. On second thought, don't. Let me keep doing your job. I'm getting paid plenty to do it, after all.)

Oh—and don't let any older person fool you into believing it's a generational thing. "This video-game-playing generation of kids," a haughty old person says, "it's a generation that can't write." "It's because they don't read enough," another snooty grown-up will add. Well, I do read, and the letters to the editors of newspapers these adults (of all ages— from barely-older-than-us, just-out-of-college adults to doddering old folks) write are riddled with the same subject-verb disagreements, the same tense confusion, the same COMMA SPLICES as the papers my peers write and that I write for my peers. Their transitions between ideas aren't any clearer, either.

If you read enough, do so carefully, and know what to look for, though, figuring out what a D paper should look like versus a C or a B isn't that difficult. English teachers are just experienced readers. They've read a lot of pretty decent student writing and even more hasty, careless writing, and they're good at shoving essays into assessment drawers. You do the same thing with clothing. You put all of your socks together in one drawer because they all have similar characteristics. They look the same and feel the same. You don't look at a sock and wonder, "Is that a sweater? Which drawer should I put it in?" You don't get the two confused. English teachers don't confuse D papers with B papers, either. They know what a D paper looks like, and they know what a B paper looks like. An A paper's a little different. No two true A papers look alike—and yet teachers know one when they see one. I know these things, too; I've just figured out a way to make a lot more money knowing how to read papers than teachers do.

If you want to know the truth, you probably don't need to read this entire book if all you want to do is write A papers. You can skip ahead to the section I'll write later.* And I'll give you a preview here.** It only takes me 292 words to explain how to write a strong essay. Here goes:

An essay is like a burrito. Seriously. And not just any burrito. A Chipotle burrito—the world's best, most perfect food. You start by laying out the surface on which your essay will build. That's your introduction. Your tortilla. You often have a pretty good idea what the ingredients will be—you have examples in mind, points you want to make—but often something else, or something different, catches your eye. A new point. An ingredient you hadn't been thinking of that all of a sudden strikes you as more interesting, more appealing. You plan to go with chicken, maybe, but then the person ahead of you orders steak, and then when your burrito builder turns to you, you find yourself saying, "Yeah—I'll have steak, too," even though you've never had steak before.

---

* Then again, learning what D, C, and B papers look like might help you "separate the wheat from the chaff." That's an old-fart saying. It applies to doing just about anything well. For instance, drafting basketball players in the NBA. Of course, I'm a Timberwolves fan, so I've seen a whole lot of chaff and not much wheat.

** Likewise, if you have no interest in writing A papers, you can skip this preview. I'm sure I'll start to talk all teachery. I do plan to give you lots of examples that I, at least, find funny. As always, in writing and life, it's your call.

There are so many options, always, so many potential combinations. And here's the thing, the most delicious part of it all: By the time you wrap it up (your conclusion, the tortilla again, now pulling the whole thing together), the essay/burrito has become greater than the sum of its parts. Steak—yum. Peppers and onions—scrumptious. Cilantro-lime rice—mouthwateringly tasty. Same thing for corn and tomatoes and cheese. Wrap them all together with a tortilla, though (an introduction that sets the stage for alchemy, a conclusion that brings it all together in surprising, satisfying ways), and you have something *kraptaculous* (a word my grandpa used to say all the time and that should mean something's bad but instead means something's better than good because my grandpa was awesome). You've written something strong and insightful and unpredictable yet carefully constructed: something kraptaculous. Something that's gooey, chewy, and crunchy all at once. And who wouldn't want to read/eat that? Huh?

See? That's 292 words, and you have a pretty good idea—a visual, tangible, olfactorily-pleasing example—of what an essay should do and look like.

Or maybe that burrito analogy doesn't help you. If not, here's another one:

An essay is like a pitcher in baseball dueling a batter. He throws one pitch—one he thinks will work—and then throws the next one based on how the batter responded to the first one. If the batter swung ahead of the fastball and fouled it off, the pitcher might then throw a change-up that drops out of the zone in front of the batter's next swing. That's like you, in an essay, writing one sentence, considering how it feels when you read it back to yourself, and then building on it with another sentence.

How was that one? No? Not a sports fan? Okay, look at it this way: An essay is like a stand-up comedian's story. Take this example:

"Your toes just called. They want a pedicure."

I was driving through town the other day and I came to a sign at Accolades Salon that said, "Your toes just called. They want a pedicure."

As far as I knew, my toes weren't capable of picking a potato chip off the floor. (I've tried.) And now here they were punching ten buttons on a telephone and holding a conversation without my knowing it.

Apparently, my toes grabbed my phone out of my front pocket. The kinesthesia is hard to imagine here.

It seems my leg's in on it, too. I wonder if my toes complained to my leg:

MY TOES: Can you believe Charles? He still has one of those old flip phones. Do you know how hard that makes it to make a call?

MY LEG: I guess.

MY TOES: This would be a lot easier if he had a smart phone with big buttons on the screen.

This thought—my toes talking to my leg—scares

me. Anyway, I don't know that I want my body parts talking to each other.

I get to thinking this explains a lot, like that day in gym class in sixth grade, when my nose told my butt to fart the same time my nosed sneezed. I was sitting there, almost five feet tall, noticing that my T-shirt was longer than my shorts when I sat, and my body parts were conspiring against me.

MY NOSE: Okay, ready? I'll get started and he'll never expect you.

MY BUTT: 3, 2, 1 . . .

Blast off from both ends.

It took a month for anyone in sixth grade to forget this.

Apparently my body parts are vindictive.

And they talk to everyone but me, which made me feel lonely the afternoon I noticed the Accolades sign, even as the girl at the pedicure place finished brushing on pink sparkly nail polish.

When telling a story, the stand-up comedian needs to grab the audience's attention right away with an interesting setup or situation. Then he explores that setup or situation one beat at a time, helping the audience see the world through his eyes and building evidence toward something that seems, I don't know, important or amusing. By the end, the comedian often moves the audience somewhere surprising (such as his sitting in a salon obliging his toes' request for a pedicure). All of this is true for many *good* essays, too. As an essay writer, you get to be the comedian; you get to build your joke/essay toward a destination even you don't know until you get there.

Does that analogy help? You might also start thinking about what your essay will feel like to your reader. What effect does it have? I'll give you a couple examples of what it *might* feel like. Here's one: To your reader, a good essay should feel like an unexpected thank-you card.

> *Dear Mike, Cindy, Robert, Susie, and who could forget your darling poodle Ginger!*
>
> *I want to thank you for the beautiful belongings we stole from you last month! I'm sure you've dealt with your share of fear and trepidation since that Tuesday night we broke into your house, tied you to chairs, and wiped your place clean, but I can assure you the effort was not in vain. I can tell you we have appreciated the flat screen TV during this exciting football season!*
>
> *One of my colleagues has especially taken to the family photos, which he takes into the bathroom with him. . . . And of course we got great use out of Ginger's brother Cinnamon. He went in the Crock-Pot last week, and he fed us for three days!*
>
> *Anyway, I felt compelled to write this note of thanks as, due to the blindfolds, you could not see the expressions of glee on our faces as we robbed you of your possessions.*

> *We'll see you soon—actually we see you right*
> *now!—and you may or may not see us soon, as well!*
> *Love,*
> *the Guys*
>
> ** I say "I'm sure" because we continue to monitor*
> *your every move!*

Unexpected thank-you cards may startle a reader. They may make her reevaluate things. That's what a good essay should do, too.

You can think about it this way, as well: An essay, to your reader, should feel like an overheard conversation—one he can't stop listening to even if he has other things to do and shouldn't be there in the first place. Imagine, for instance, the audit of a niche company.

Satanic Sound Systems Audit

AUDITOR: So, Mr. . . . Mr. . . .

PROPRIETOR: Luckless.

AUDITOR: Right, Mr. Luckless. You do indeed run
    Satanic Sound Systems?

PROPRIETOR: That's right.

AUDITOR: And you specialize in . . .

PROPRIETOR: Supervillain mask sound systems.

AUDITOR: Yes. That's what I have written down
    here. I do have a few questions.

PROPRIETOR: Shoot. [Nervous twitch.] Well, no,
    don't shoot me. But ask your questions.

AUDITOR: First of all, thank you for submitting your receipts and records so readily. I hope that you don't mind that my assistant here is recording our conversation in her notepad.

PROPRIETOR: No problem. Whatever makes this process more *efficient.*

AUDITOR: It's just that it seems your business has had only three customers in forty years.

PROPRIETOR: Yes, that's right. They're powerful customers, you see. [Peers over the auditor's shoulder to the street, looking nervously for someone.] Is there any way we can speed this up?

AUDITOR: Now hold on a minute, Mr. Luckless. This is important record-keeping work. I see here that you did submit your customers' names. Let me see here: Saki, Oroku, nicknamed "Shredder"; Vader, Darth; and Bane ... am I missing a last name for that one?

PROPRIETOR: No. He's never revealed one. Not to me, anyway.

AUDITOR: Will it be possible for you to obtain this customer's—Bane's—last name?

PROPRIETOR: I'd really rather not ask him.

AUDITOR: Surely you have his last name through credit card charge slips?

PROPRIETOR: My customers don't pay with credit cards. [Looks over auditor's shoulder again.] Listen: Perhaps we can continue this conversation via email?

AUDITOR: You sell expensive machinery here, Mr. Luckless. Do you mean to tell me your customers pay in *cash?*

PROPRIETOR: They . . . they don't really pay at all.

AUDITOR: And yet you've remained in business all these years?

PROPRIETOR: Whenever the business needs funding, or . . . or anything, these customers . . . they make it happen.

AUDITOR: What do you mean "make it happen"?

PROPRIETOR: . . .

AUDITOR: It says here, Mr. Luckless, that Satanic Sound Systems has been audited three times previously?

PROPRIETOR: Yes.

AUDITOR: I can't find the records from those audits, however.

PROPRIETOR: . . . Maybe you should return to your office? We could finish over the phone?

AUDITOR: Just one minute, Mr. Luckless, and we'll be done. I'm here already—no use in interrupting the process now.

PROPRIETOR: . . .

AUDITOR: Perhaps I could trace down your previous auditors. Can you describe those auditors to me, their physical appearances?

PROPRIETOR: [Mumbling.] Broken neck, suffocation with no marks, broken back.

AUDITOR: Excuse me—
Glass storefront crashes to the floor.
AUDITOR: What the . . . ? What was that?
PROPRIETOR: My customers. I'm sorry, Mr. . . . ?
Mr. . . . ? I never remember to get your names.

Like an overheard conversation, a good essay should feel dangerous somehow. As if the subject matter is so important or scary or relevant to the reader that she can't stop reading.

Why have I given you all of these analogies? How can an essay be like a burrito, a pitcher in baseball dueling a batter, a stand-up comedian's joke,☼ an unexpected thank-you card, and an overheard conversation all at the same time? Well, it can be like a football or soccer game, too, or a good movie, or a great party. Whatever you like to do and take the time to do right, chances are an essay is like that. I guess the thing that's helped me most these last four years was realizing early on that pretty much everything in life is like writing an essay. Start to see everything you do as an essay, and then the whole writing thing makes a lot more sense. Most things you like to do, you don't need to know exactly how they're going to turn out ahead of time,

---

☼ So three of my examples in this preview were, I hope you noticed, funny—or were meant to be. If you're serious about learning to write A essays (which means you're serious about *really* writing), then you might try writing something funny (at least to you) every day. Really. I can't think of any better way to develop personality in your prose. That, and cadence, and rhythm, and the patience to write one sentence at a time and appreciate that it builds toward something.

right? You just make choices as you go and see what happens.° What's similar about all of these analogies? Well, a good essay happens one sentence at a time. You don't usually start knowing how it will end. Instead, you start somewhere interesting, such as in front of the Chipotle burrito line or in a room overhearing a conversation between an auditor and a guy who sells sound systems to supervillains. Then each choice you make and each piece of evidence you learn clarifies or complicates the situation until you pave your way to a conclusion that satisfies and likely surprises even, especially, you. Sometimes when you write an essay, you don't even begin at the beginning. You know what's going to go in the middle first, so you start there. No matter where you are in the paper, the writing process happens one sentence at a time. If you can't get lost in your head enough to end up in places you didn't predict, you aren't really writing. Even as I write all of this down for you, I've lost track of time. And for me, time is money. Yeah—you're welcome.

Later on, I'll let you sit with me as I write an A essay. It won't be pretty—the process, I mean. I won't always know what I'm doing or what to write next. But I'll end up, I hope, with something that actually feels honest to me and worth someone's time to read.

○ I'm always hearing people talk about *writer's block*. I don't get that. What do you do in life that doesn't require you to think occasionally? And if you're so stuck—so blocked—why keep doing it? Why not move on to something that does make sense. In writing, that's a new part of the paper or a new topic altogether.

That said, in this book I'm teaching you not only how to write A essays but how to make money, and that will mean writing all kinds of essays, from putrid to passable to pulchritudinous (don't know what that means? Sorry—I needed another word with a P. Look it up), then read on.

Okay, so here's my formula. Or part of the formula. I've already gotten carried away and spent more time working on this blueprint and supplying you with examples than I had scheduled. I still need to keep up my business, and that means I need to write eleven essays before I go to bed tonight, in addition to attending my classes and then hunting down Marc Pride. Honestly, I don't know why I'm writing this share-all book anymore. I hope you appreciate it. Anyway, here's one example essay—a D-plus essay. Tomorrow, Wednesday, I'll show you a C-plus essay. Thursday, a B-plus essay. I'll save the A for Friday, when I can stay up later and devote an entire afternoon to it. Believe me—A essays require that kind of time.

The D-Plus Paper

This D-plus essay deals with S. E. Hinton's *The Outsiders*, the first book we read in ninth grade, the book I mentioned earlier because it was passed around in secret by teenage readers, which should be a lesson to us all. The instructions for the essay: *Write a one-and-a-half-page essay in which you make and support some claim regarding the novel* The Outsiders.

You've seen assignments like this, right? If you want to write a D paper on something like this, begin by not reading the assignment expectations very closely.

Any true D-plus paper does the following:

- Fails to fulfill the assignment guidelines.
- Disregards expectations of English language structure.
- Has no title.

That's it. That's all you need to remember if you'd like to write a D-plus paper. Go ahead and write one, for practice. They don't take much time (ten minutes, max, when you've written as many of them as I have). Here's one, which I wrote for Hal Burk, who paid me five bucks.

The outsiders$_1$ is a cool book, it$_2$ has lots of violence,$_3$ (but probably not enough) The main character his name is ponyboy he$_4$ kills a guy and runs away. its kind of boring for a while when they were in the church but then the church caught on fire and that was pretty cool too I guess.

I guess i like dally the best because he's the toughest. He bashes in the socks but they probably had it coming. Maybe hes not that smart though because he robs a bank and kind of gets himself killed in the end. He did other cool stuff too though before he did that dumb thing and died.

That girl cherry she sounds pretty. She kind of betrays the socks, I bet they don't like that too much. It helps the greasers though. The rumble at the end is cool but it probably won't make any difference. It's not like the socks are going to stop being rich or anything or you know hand over their houses to the greasers. That would be cool though.

Back to ponyboy, he ended up okay and then he writes this book to cope i think. That's cool. He has two brothers and they get to be a family still at the end I think. They eat a lot of chocolate cake which would be the coolest.

My essay for Hal isn't even a full page, and it really never says anything about *The Outsiders* (except, maybe, that there's some cool stuff in the book, which is a start. If I wanted a better essay, I'd need to explain what that cool stuff is and why it's cool). Here's something to take with you: A lot of decent essays have some kind of claim or point or question at the beginning. Schools call them *thesis statements*, though there are lots of other ways to make a point or get someone's attention. As we get to the B essay and then, of course, the A essay,♪ I'll make a point of some sort at the beginning and then build on it. But Hal's essay isn't a B. There's not even one developed idea in my D-plus essay for Hal. He didn't pay for a developed idea.

And that's certainly not the only blunder in this essay. See the numbers I typed into the essay for you? Those correspond with the problems I explain below.

1. This hasn't been proofread. See the capitalization errors? The first letter of a new sentence needs to be capitalized because readers are used to seeing them this way. Your job is to make your reader's job easier and not more difficult. Plus, key words in the title of a book need to begin with capital letters. In this case, that's easy: *The Outsiders.* Notice that I italicized the title. All names need to begin with a capital letter, as well (**P**onyboy, not **p**onyboy; **C**herry, not **c**herry). The first-person pronoun *I* always needs to be capitalized. I'm sure you know this and just don't take the time to proofread your work—but you should start taking the time, at least if a higher grade or simply the quality of your writing matters to you. Teachers and their grade books don't usually forgive you for overlooking some of these basic courtesies to your reader, and they shouldn't.

♪ Please provide your own sound track. I hope every time you read "the A essay" you hear heroic music. Something from one of those superhero blockbusters released every summer teachers at my high school believe we all see (because we do).

2. Take a look at the confusing punctuation. The essay BEGINS with a comma splice. Did I mention that comma splices make me dry heave? *"The Outsiders* is a cool book" could be its own sentence, right? And so could "It has lots of violence," right? Each clause has a subject (a something) and a predicate (something the subject does), right? Then you can't leave a comma alone there. You could write, instead, *"The Outsiders* is a cool book. It has lots of violence." There I used a period. Or you could write, *"The Outsiders* is a cool book <u>because</u> it has lots of violence." But a scrawny little comma can't stand on its own between those two independent clauses. Imagine, again, a tiny wide receiver trying to block two huge defensive linemen. They'd bend him like a comma, wouldn't they? You need a strong, stocky fullback to muscle in there and help. If this fullback makes the comma a semicolon, the sentence works: *"The Outsiders* is a cool book; it has lots of violence." See the dot on top of the comma? Now the comma's a semicolon. Think of the dot on top of the comma (now a semicolon) as the strong, stocky fullback who runs into the middle of the sentence to help the scrawny wide receiver block the 300-pound defensive ends. Some people say a picture is worth a thousand words. I don't know what that means. Why a thousand? Why not ten words, or fifty thousand? I don't get it. In case you do, here's my attempt to draw what I mean:

See? The wide receiver bends between the linemen like a comma does between two independent clauses. Not as technical as it sounds, right?

The fullback makes the comma a semicolon and together they block the linemen.

44

A semicolon *can* support two independent clauses on its own, though not for long: If you have two long independent clauses that aren't very closely related, you're better off with a period. Imagine two serpentine trains that don't have much in common—perhaps the Hogwarts Express and the Orient Express—on the same tracks and careening toward each other. You need more than even a semicolon to prevent their collision. You need a more forceful barrier. You need a period. Fine—another drawing (look at page 46).

3. Okay—back to my notes on the D-plus paper. I need to push that first period to *after* the stuff in parentheses. I have it like this: ". . . it has lots of violence. (but should probably have more)" while it should say, "it has lots of violence (but should probably have more)." The period goes *after* the parenthetical because what's inside the parentheses is part of this thought/sentence and not the next one.

4. To make sure this looked like a D essay, I also added unnecessary words—words that only make the reader's job more difficult. Take this sentence, for instance: "The main character <u>his name is ponyboy he</u> kills a guy and runs away." See all those extra words in the middle? If I want an essay worth more than a D-plus, I might write, "The main character, Ponyboy, kills a guy and runs away."

There's too much going on here for even a

I know I just threw a lot at you. It's all the stuff you hate sitting through in an English class, right? But if you're serious about making money writing essays, it's stuff you need to know. Or maybe it does all make sense right now. If not, you can go back and reread this section whenever you want.

On to content. Where are the specific examples from the text? I (as Hal) mention some events from the book, but I don't spend any time with these events and explain why the reader should know about them. It can help to quote from the book, though you don't want to overdo this, either. Oh, and a writer needs to get his facts straight! Ponyboy doesn't kill Bob the Soc, as this essay suggests; Johnny kills Bob. This is yet another trait of the D-plus essay: The writer doesn't take the time to understand what she read.

Writing this D-plus essay couldn't have taken very long, you say? The answer: No—it didn't. It took ten minutes.[*] *Why didn't Hal just write this for himself and save the money?* Well, I don't judge my customers. I get it. People have better things to do than write rushed essays. This sorry excuse for an essay would have been a waste of *my* time, too, if it hadn't earned me five dollars.

So there you have it: a D-plus essay.

---

[*] This is how long it takes me, not you. I get that. I've been writing hundreds of papers each semester for years now. You might not get as much done as I do in ten minutes. Still, you'll see that a D-plus won't take you as long as a C-plus.

* * * * *

I spend the day at school looking over my shoulder. I always knew, of course, that someone would be assigned to eliminate me, but now it's real. Plus, this person's good. He followed me into the trees yesterday, when I was certain no one had seen me, and nearly took care of me there. I have to be careful.

And yet I have my own mission, too.

It's now 3:05, and the next hour (what I have before I need to start writing essays) won't be all hiding. Today is Marc Pride's reckoning.

I know he's mowing a lawn this afternoon. I know this because I write his essays for him. He pays for Bs, which means he had to self-audit and then present to me his financial situation, with promises of potential and stability. What I don't know is whose lawn he mows Tuesday afternoons immediately after school.

I maneuver through hallway traffic on my way to the locker bay near the history classrooms. Before I get there, Max Latterly grabs my backpack and yanks me to his locker. He's a bulky guy who plays hockey and already has a receding hairline, not to mention a shrunken brain. He pays for Cs, and I'm not sure his business is worth the trouble.

"Dremmel!" Max shouts, though my face is inches from his. "What's the deal with those Blue Book exams, huh? How we gonna pull that one off?"

Someone says, "Not so loud, Max," but a small

crowd gathers around me, wanting to hear my answer to Max's question. Max looks behind him to admire the crowd, and I break for it, shoving my classmates out of the way as I mutter, "I'm working on it."

I begin to dart in and out of traffic like Barry Sanders in 1997 (YouTube it) as Max shouts, "I wasn't through talking to you, Dremmel!"

I shout back, "Yeah, but I was through talking to you!"

At the locker bay outside the history classrooms, I find my best friend Doug, who has advisory with Marc Pride.

I shove him into his locker with both hands, the way we've greeted each other ever since I can remember. He turns, recognizes me, and shoves me back into the middle of the hall.

"Chuckles," ≈ he says. "What's happening?"

"Not much."

"Hey—do you know where I might find Marc Pride?"

"Mowing a lawn, I'm sure."

"Yeah, I figured. Any chance he told you which one?"

Doug thinks about this. "He said in advisory he'd be at the Logans. He likes mowing their lawn because they don't have many trees but they still pay a fair price. Anyway, that's what he said. Why?"

I ignore Doug's question. "Thanks. Gotta run."

≈ Okay—so my friend's name is not really Doug, and he doesn't really call me Chuckles (because my name's not Charles). But I really do have a best friend and he really does call me a nickname no one else does. I wish that for everybody—a best friend and a nickname.

I walk all the way through the athletic hallway to the exit near the gym to make sure no one follows me.

The Logans live on the other side of town, and I need to take the bus. I'm in a rush, as always, because as much as I want to win the Nerf War this year, I still have essay deadlines to meet. The bus passes restaurants, shops, the library, churches, and a synagogue. As I ride, I narrate (in my head) my surroundings. The man next to me smells like BOTH deodorant and sweaty armpits. The woman across from me taps her foot. She must be in a hurry to get wherever she's going. Or maybe she's nervous, not so sure she wants to get there at all? She stands up suddenly, before the bus stops, and takes two steps closer to the door, grabbing a pole for balance. Yep— she's in a hurry. The bus bounces over a speed bump and jars us passengers as if we're on the Enterprise's bridge and the ship's been struck by a photon torpedo. I narrate in this way—in my head—as often as possible. These are my Thought Farts, if only I had a pen and paper, and I curse myself for not having these out. Even without writing these thoughts down, though, narrating them helps my writing. I'm practicing noticing; practicing creating sentences; practicing thinking.

I get off two blocks from the Logans' house and walk the rest of the way, holding my Quick 16 Blaster close to my body. I walk carefully, sticking to trees and hedges whenever possible, and when I get close enough to see Marc mowing the lawn, I realize I've been overly cautious. He has his shirt off, his sunglasses on, and he's listening to music through an iPhone, the cord of his earplugs snaking like a vine down his left side into the left front pocket of his blue basketball shorts.

He's bobbing his head to the music and watching the lawn in front of him as he pushes the lawn mower toward me. When he turns, I jog up to him from two lawns down and shoot him in the back. On some late-night TV show I once heard Clint Eastwood tell a story about John Wayne, how he would never shoot a person in the back in any of his movies. I respect that sense of killing etiquette, and I feel bad about peppering Marc's back with Nerf darts. I feel bad until I see him scratching his back without turning around or looking over his shoulder. He must think a couple bugs bit him. I shout after him, "Marc—I hit you! You're eliminated!" but he keeps pushing his lawn mower away from me, my words unable to penetrate the noise of the lawn mower and the iPhone's music. When he reaches the edge of the lawn, pivots the lawn mower, and heads back in my direction, he still doesn't see me right away.

I wave my hands like an idiot and shout, "MARC! MARC!" He looks up, notices me, grins, and pushes the lawn mower closer to me.

"Charles," he says. "What are you doing here?" That's when I hear a sound—something besides blades of grass chewed up by the lawn mower.

My darts. Five of them.

I lift my Quick 16 Blaster feebly and repeat, "I— uh—I hit you, Marc."

He looks confused at first, and then he gets it. "Oh, right! The Nerf War. Man—you came all the way out here to get me. Nice."

"Yeah." I feel foolish. "So—can I have your index card?"

"Yeah, yeah. Of course. Hold on." He pulls the lawn mower's lever into neutral and strolls over to the Logans' front steps. His backpack's there, and he digs through it. He returns empty-handed.

"Charles—I'm sorry, man. I have no idea where that is. Maybe in my locker at school?"

I curse under my breath. "Can you tell me whose name was on it?"

"Sorry again. I'm not sure I ever read it. Just too busy these days, you know?"

I don't know, but what can I do? I nod.

When I step back onto the bus stop, I understand that my primary objective now is to avoid getting caught. Hopefully Marc will find the index card soon or I'll figure something else out. I don't have any more time to spend on this today.

Wednesday, March 3

Last night: More panicked calls and messages lead-ing to fitful sleep and horrific dreams. I replaced the Jaws text-message music with "Softly Crashing Waves." I woke three times feeling seasick, coughing up imaginary water. Staying awake in school will be a challenge today, but I do need to remain alert—to avoid conversations about Blue Book exams and to hopefully pick up whatever I can about the Nerf War sniper on my tail.

The C-Plus Paper

A C-plus essay is really pretty similar to a D-plus essay; it just gets closer to fulfilling the assignment and is a bit easier to read. It has a title, but that title is usually something monumentally unoriginal like "English Essay."

English Essay

The Outsiders is an interesting book. I admit, I especially like the violence. The main character, Ponyboy, gets jumped by Socs at the beginning of the novel. He remembers shortly after that his friend Johnny got jumped recently too. And then they get jumped together not long after that. This time it's different, though, this time they kill one of the Socs, which means they need to run away.

It's kind of boring for a while when they were in the church♣ but then the church caught on fire and that was when things picked up I guess. Oh, and before that Dally arrived and he's tough, which makes him interesting to watch. He's always talking about bashing in the Socs and it's difficult not to root for him because the Socs probably have it coming. Dally's probably not that smart, though, because he robs a bank and kind of gets himself killed in the end.

There's a girl named Cherry who's very pretty. After Bob (her boyfriend) gets killed, she surprises everyone by helping the greasers. She knows that "Bob asked for it" (Hinton 128). So she tells the greasers what kind of weapons the Socs will bring to the rumble near the end of the book. The rumble at the end is cool but it probably won't make any difference. It's not like the Socs are going to stop being rich or anything. They won't hand over the keys to their houses to the greasers.

Ponyboy sometimes says the smartest things in the book. He realizes before the rumble that "'Greaser didn't have anything to do with it,'" he's talking about saving kids from the church fire (117). It really bothers him that people fight for no reason. He ends up writing his book to cope with it. He seems to be okay at the end, it helps that he has two brothers and they get to be a family still. They have a really tight bond.

This one's over a page, once the writer includes name, teacher, class, and date information in the upper left corner. It still doesn't meet the page-and-half requirement, and it still doesn't make a clear claim about *The Outsiders*, but teachers don't like giving Ds unless something's beyond putrid (like Hal's essay). They feel that a D grade discourages the writer. I don't understand this logic. Earning a D would only discourage me if I'd spent enough time (twenty minutes) to earn a C. If I spent less time than that, I was obviously striving for a D.

The writing's more efficient in the C paper, which means the writer wastes fewer words. In this C-plus essay, you see two quoted examples from the text, which help support the points made in those paragraphs.

Those quotations also show readers that the writer has attempted to read *The Outsiders* carefully and pay attention to what's on each page.

There's a lot to improve here, though. See the moldy, good-for-nothing comma splices? Here's one: "This time it's different, thou<u>gh, t</u>his time they kill one of the Socs, which means they need to run away." "This time it's different, though" could stand on its own as a complete sentence, right? And so could "This time they kill one of the Socs, which means they need to run away." That means the comma I've underlined should be a period or a semicolon (remember the strong stocky fullback?). Here's another one: "He seems to be okay at the <u>end, it</u> helps that he has two brothers and they get to be a family still." If this hasn't sunk in yet, go back to the illustration on page 43. You can't expect a wide receiver to block two defensive linemen, and you can't expect a comma to support two independent clauses. I swear at the computer screen as I type comma-spliced sentences, but I know my classmates would write them, and I want my essay forgeries to feel authentic. And as long as I get paid, I can live (just barely) with typing a few (hundred) comma splices.

I marked the first sentence of the second paragraph with a shamrock (♣). See it? Notice that it has only three leaves and not four, as it does NOT bring grading good luck. This clover marks a problem most C papers have: Their verbs switch tenses in confusing ways. **Remain in present tense when writing about books** unless it absolutely doesn't make sense anymore. Here the sentence could say, "It's kind of boring for a while when they *are* in the church." That way, both verbs (*It's* and *are*) share a present tense.

Is this getting too technical for you? Well, if you don't care about these things, you can't write essays that are like burritos—at least not ones that taste scrumptious to the reader, too—and you certainly can't run an essay-writing business.

✳ ✳ ✳ ✳ ✳

I ask Ms. Oversand if I can leave science three minutes early. I tell her I've finished my lab and need to use the bathroom. She excuses me.

I get to Doug's locker before he does. He's agreed to give me a ride home to help protect me in the Nerf War. He thinks it's pretty funny, actually.

"Chuckles," he says as he joins me at his locker and spins the lock. "You really want to win this thing, don't you?"

"You know I do," I reply.

"Explain to me why it's so important. Just never thought this big social game would be your thing."

"Yeah, I don't know." As I've told you, that's the truth. I have no idea why this matters to me. I never knew I cared about anything going on at this high school, or even my legacy, until the last couple months. The idea just grabbed hold of me. "I guess I just don't like the idea of someone getting the better of me. Anyway, thanks for the ride."

"No problem. We just need to make it quick. I've got baseball practice in half an hour."

"Believe me—I don't want to hang around here longer than I need to." I pull up my sweatshirt's hood to hide my face.

On the way out, I spot Marc Pride. His back is to us and he's talking to someone I can't see.

"Hey, Doug," I say. "Give me a second. I'm going to see if Marc has found his index card." At lunch, I told Doug about my trip to the Logans' yesterday. "I'll be fast about it."

Doug nods, and I slip across the hallway.

I say, "Marc," and he turns to face me. When he does, I see who he's talking to. Lisa Kent. Yeah, Lisa Kent with the big brown eyes, which are looking at me now. I get lost in them for a moment, and then Marc's voice yanks me back the way Max Latterly's strong arm did yesterday.

"Charles?"

"Hey," I say, knowing that's not enough. We stand in silence. I don't look at Lisa, but I know she's there. Suddenly I feel stupid, stopping their conversation to ask about Nerf War, and I wonder what Lisa would think about it, and about me playing it.♥ I feel awkward

---

♥ I know, I know. Why should I care what she thinks? I mean, I do write A essays for her for free. One guy wrote, a long time ago, that "Love makes fools of us all." In other words, forget you, Lisa Kent.

and immature as I remember the plastic gun in my backpack.

Marc breaks the silence. "If you're looking for that index card, my man, I'm sorry. I still haven't found it."

"Uh . . . never mind." In my hurry to get away from this conversation, I nearly back into Doug, who's come up behind me. "Whoa," he says quietly, grabbing my shoulders.

Doug takes care of the social interaction for me. "Hey, Marc, Lisa," he says. "We heard you were in some play, Lisa, at the State Theater? Aren't you playing like two parts?"

She smiles. Doug's always had a way. "Yeah—*Hamlet*. It's pretty avant-garde. You guys should come."

A part of me—the stupid, dumb, Neanderthal part—thinks, *She's asking me to watch her play!* Yep, it's "You make me laugh. I hope we have a class together next year" in my yearbook all over again.

"Sounds awesome," Doug says. He looks at me with his eyebrows raised. Nudges me with his shoulder. Oh. I'm supposed to say something.

"Yeah," I mutter. "Awesome."

Doug has the decency to hold his laughter until we're in his car.

Thursday, March 4

This morning, I stumble out my front door and down the front steps, lost in thought, and there they are. Thirteen of my classmates standing on the sidewalk, waiting for me. Some of them have letterman jackets on, yet another indication that it's not spring yet and they don't need to bother me about those Blue Books. Standing there looking menacing in their letterman jackets, they have no idea how much they resemble the Socs from those *Outsiders* essays I wrote for them.

I close my eyes and rub my temples. The sound of "Softly Crashing Waves" enters my brain, and I cough instinctively.

"Seriously," I say, "you all need to get lives."

"Dremmel," says Chris Rinkles, stepping forward. "Uh, good morning. We were wondering if you know what's going to happen with those Blue Books yet."

I stare at them. It's too early for me to be civil, so I keep my mouth shut.

Chris speaks again: "It's just that, you know, well—we're worried about college. We don't want to get caught and get, well, kicked out before we even start."

I talk without thinking. "You know, if you all would have just taken the time to write your own papers, you wouldn't have anything to worry about."

Max Latterly steps forward. "What's that, Dremmel? Thing is, if we go down, you do, too." And then he pulls his own Quick 16 Blaster from behind his back and pumps out sixteen shots. Eight miss, but the damage has been done. I'm out of the Nerf War. Max raises the gun above his head, turns to the others, and says, "I've been wanting to do that to the dork all week." I'm so stunned and disappointed I don't move for what might be a long time. When Max turns back to me, he says, "Next time it's my fist and your face, Dremmel."

Chris steps between us. "Easy now, Max. We're just talking."

I climb backward and up until I'm at the top of the front steps, so I can see and address everyone. But I just had one of the two parts to my legacy murdered, and I don't feel like talking. I certainly don't care about their Blue Book exams right now. I suppose the only road to take is the high road. "Sorry, Max—I don't have an index card. My last target couldn't find his," I say.

Max looks confused. More confused than usual, even. He squints, and we can all see the gears in his brain slowly turning. Finally, he says, "I don't want your card, Dremmel. I didn't do that for the Nerf War. I need to shoot someone else for that. I just couldn't help myself." He laughs. He raises his closed left hand, looking for a fist bump. No one pays any attention. While it takes a moment for the news to sink in—that I'm still alive in the War—when it does I wake up with more strength than I've had all morning. I raise my voice to address my audience.

"Max is right," I announce. "About what he said before, I mean. We're in this together. So you need to trust that I have a plan. Unless you can think of some other option. Now I'm going to walk to school, and not with you all. I need time with my thoughts so I can write the papers you have due in the next three months. You just keep giving me your Thought Farts and quit worrying so much. It will all probably work out."

I cut through our front lawn to a spot in the sidewalk well ahead of the mob. I hear someone say, "Did he say *probably*?" Nobody chases after me, though, and I know I'm still in control, both in my essay-writing business and, amazingly, in the Nerf War.

After first period, I see Lisa Kent at her locker and she waves and smiles. Even after yesterday, she wants to talk to me? My breath catches, and I'm about to wave back when Tina Quimbley squeezes past me and says, "Lisa—you're never gonna guess what just happened."

I know what happened, though. Lisa was waving to her friend and not her Jay Gatsby. Her Mario.

Figures.

✳ ✳ ✳ ✳ ✳

The B-Plus Paper

If you're still reading, that means you're interested in writing B papers—for yourself or for profit. (Either that or you care as much as I do about this school's Nerf War and my fate in it.) I applaud your ambition. But if you want to write B papers, you need to know you're in for quite a bit of work. A B or B-plus paper is a significant step forward from a C-plus. Find some comfort in this, however: *The B is an English teacher's favorite grade.* It tells a student, "Hey—you put some real thought into this. You made a claim at the beginning, and then you supported it." "You completed the assignment," a B says, "and you paid attention to the expectations. Good for you." A B also says, "Here are some things to work on." A teacher might remind you to keep enhancing your writing vocabulary, especially your verbs, or to fully develop an idea or allusion. Perhaps she'll write a note at the end that some figurative language would help you show readers what you mean. She'll likely remind you to show instead of tell. Or, depending on the assignment, to both show *and* tell.

That's what I'm doing here, after all—showing you and telling you what a B-plus paper looks like.

Okay, the B-plus paper:

Stick Together

At the beginning of S.E. Hinton's *The Outsiders*, the narrator and protagonist, Ponyboy Curtis, gets jumped by several rich kids he calls Socs. Nearly instantly, his brothers and buddies are there to help him and comfort him. This gang of greasers, as they call themselves, has become a family. They're there for each other. We get the sense, as readers, that as long as the main characters in *The Outsiders* stick together, they'll be okay.

Together, they've endured the tragic death of the Curtis boys' parents. They've endured Johnny's parents beating him and Two-Bit's mother working long hours as a barmaid (Hinton 43). It's when they don't stick together that things go wrong.

Ponyboy tells us that Johnny got jumped recently when he hung out by himself in the lot. There's Ponyboy's incident at the beginning of the book, too, as he walks home alone from a movie, something he admits he shouldn't do. Finally, when Ponyboy argues with his brother Darry and runs away to the park with Johnny, they find themselves surrounded by Socs. These Socs nearly drown Ponyboy before Johnny stabs and kills one of them (56). They go to their friend Dally, who gives them bad advice:

Run away. At the time, it doesn't feel like such bad advice, but in hindsight we want to yell, "No! Stay with your brothers, Ponyboy! They'll help you through this." While they become heroes after running away because they save young children from a burning church, they also get sick, and then Johnny breaks his back during the rescue.

Dally probably supports my thesis best. He's always been the loner in the group, the one who never gets attached to anyone. Who lives by his own rules. He tells Ponyboy, "You look out for yourself and nothin' can touch you" (147). In the end, though, Dally robs a grocery store and runs out into the night with a gun because he wants the police to shoot him. He runs off on his own, and he's not strong enough on his own to continue living. This scene provides a stark contrast: the entire gang stands together; they've run to find Dally. And then there's Dally, at a distance, alone. They can't get to him in time. He believes there's no reason to keep on living. If only the gang could have made it to him and embraced him, he may have endured.

Ponyboy seems to be okay at the end. He has his brothers. They look out for each other. They love each other. They even cook for each other—even if it is only mushroom soup and chocolate cake (158, 105). As long as they stick together, they'll make it work.

This B-plus paper meets the one-and-a-half page length requirement. It makes a claim—yep, here it's a *thesis statement*—at the end of the introductory paragraph: "We get the sense, as readers, that as long as the main characters in *The Outsiders* stick together, they'll be okay." This statement lets readers know what point the essay intends to prove or support.

In this B-plus essay, examples from the book—both quoted and merely cited—demonstrate careful reading. This essay bears proof of time spent thinking (thirty-five minutes). The organization of the content seems to make sense.

Five sturdy paragraphs here guide the reader: an introduction, three body paragraphs, and a conclusion. Ever heard of the five-paragraph essay? It's a perfectly legitimate formula, one this essay uses effectively. **Do keep in mind, though, that an A essay requires more than following a formula**. Some writers believe in the five-paragraph essay format like they believe in taking off their shoes before they go to bed. "It's the *right* thing to do," they tell themselves. I agree, of course. It *is* the right thing to do—if you want a B-plus. If you want to do a perfectly acceptable, reasonably thoughtful job on the assignment. The essay you just read provides an example of just such an essay. An A essay,♪♪ however, demands more than plugging text (even polished text) into a five-paragraph template and saying, "There. I've completed the assignment." Good writing requires adaptation. Your format needs to suit the content. That's why it takes so long to write one, and it's why A essays cost so much if I'm writing them—$100 instead of $20.

All that stuff I wrote above and below the B-plus essay, which comes straight from English teachers' pens—it's all true. I mean, they're right. The writer of my B-plus paper, if it wasn't actually me, could use stronger, more specific, more active verbs. If I hadn't written this essay, I would recommend that whoever did replace the verb phrase "his brothers and buddies *are there*" in the second sentence with "his brothers and buddies *arrive*" or "his brothers and buddies *appear*." **Strong, precise, interesting verbs often create powerfully efficient writing.♦** As you revise your work, always look for "to be" verbs—am, is, are, was, were—and consider replacing them with stronger

---

♪♪ Do you hear the heroic music? I hope so. If you put in the time to write an A essay, you deserve heroic music.

♦ I've put together a list of strong verbs used in this book. You'll find this list at the end of the book.

verbs. Weak verbs don't foretell the end of the world; in fact, sometimes they fit just right; but you do want to evaluate each one and consider if you've expressed yourself as engagingly and succinctly as you want. You might consider where figurative language would help a reader see and understand your point or point of view. How about "Dally has always considered himself a lone wolf at heart—someone who sticks with his pack to survive in a dangerous world but ultimately looks out for himself" instead of "He's always been the loner in the group—the one who never gets attached to anyone"? Making this revision would allow me, in the next sentence, to write, "He realizes he needs companionship, and that he's part of a family, too late, and he can't cope with the realization. He can't bear to live without his friend Johnny, and so he wonders off alone, the predator becoming the prey, a wounded animal shot down by men with guns."··· That's what I might have written in an A essay.

Doug gives me a ride home again after school today. He's agreed to do it the rest of the year so I can avoid customers and snipers. At lunch today, he got to witness firsthand the horrors I deal with. I barely ate three bites

---

∴ I feel for Dally. He lives a pretty miserable life, essentially alone, always with distance between him and everyone else. I can't imagine how someone could live like that.

of my peanut butter and grape jelly sandwich because after each bite, somebody, politely or not so politely, interrogated me about the Blue Books situation.

On the short drive to my house, I can tell Doug's got something on his mind, but we don't say anything. He nods at me when I get out of the car, and I nod back. Then he reverses and returns to school for his baseball practice. There, on top of the backseat, pressed against the back windshield, is Doug's own yellow Quick 16 Blaster.

And then it hits me. Is he the one who's after me? Is there no one I can trust?

Friday, March 5

I slept well last night for the first time all week. If my customers get to keep breaking the written rule about talking business at school, I get to break my own unwritten rule about always responding promptly to their every question. Before lying down last night, I silenced my cell phone. I pick it up now and see that I missed four calls and eight texts last night. There's only one name in my Missed Calls log I'm willing to call back. I remember the look he gave me in his car. The Nerf gun I saw through his back windshield.

I press 3 and then Talk on my phone, and it speed dials my best friend, Doug.

"Chuckles," he says. "What's happening?"

"So now you're on my back, too?" I say. "Calling me at eleven at night? Where's the loyalty? Listen: I have a plan for the Blue Books. It'll work out." I hope.

"Whoa. Hey—I know. It just seems like you're in a rut right now. I was wondering if you wanna play

Madden tonight or hit up the Drive-in." Or go somewhere else where you can shoot me with foam darts?

"Oh. No. I wish I could." And a part of me really does. Before ninth grade, I spent nearly every evening with Doug and other friends, playing football, basketball, baseball, or their video game equivalents. Or we'd see movies for free at Star View Drive-in, which Doug's parents own. "The business is killing me right now."

"Actually," I add, "I could use your help—with the Blue Book deal."

Doug doesn't say anything for a moment. When he does, he says this: "Sure, Chuckles. Not with the writing, right? I mean, I can't write other people's essays. I wouldn't know where to begin."

"No—not with writing anyone's essay."

"Okay then. Tell me what you need."

I tell him. He agrees to help.

"And hey," he adds, "come over tonight if you change your mind."

"Sure. We'll see." He and I both know it's not going to happen. I reserve my Friday afternoons for writing A essays and the rest of the weekend for whatever else needs writing. That might even be why Doug tends to ask me to hang out on Fridays—he knows I can't. Or maybe I'm paranoid. I don't know.

The A Paper: What You Need to Know If You
Really© Want to Write

An A essay—it's a special thing. You can't rush an A essay. Most English teachers (at least in my life and business) will forgive quite a bit when assigning a B grade. They'll ask questions about but give credit for an analogy not yet fully fleshed out. Yes, they'll even overlook the occasional comma splice. Not so with an A. Stay with me, and I'll walk you through my A-essay writing process.

I don't write many A essays. Customers can't afford them. I ask the B students before each semester if they want me to make them A students. They think about it, but Bs cost less. If someone turns in twenty A papers in a school year, she owes me two thousand dollars; if she turns in twenty B papers, she owes me four hundred dollars. (Does twenty papers sound like a lot? Remember, I count any piece of writing assigned by an English or history teacher and worked on outside of class. Perhaps twenty dollars for an extended paragraph sounds expensive. It all balances out, though, as a five- or seven-page paper for twenty becomes a steal for the customer.) Clearly, it adds up. And a B still plops her onto an honor roll, providing her parents with a bumper sticker they're proud of, which makes her choice easier. If her teacher

---

© I used a copyright symbol for a footnote here because the A paper requires pedal-to-the-metal, no-holds-barred, original work. If you want to write A papers, you need to put everything you have, for a few hours (at least), into that paper. Sorry. It's just the way the universe works. Read on only if you're up to the task; otherwise, it'll be a waste of your time.

gives a lot of points for other types of homework or class participation, my client may still end the grading term with an A-minus even after turning in all B papers (that she didn't write). Heck, I turn in (and write) B papers for myself as a cover. No teacher would ever suspect comma-splicing me to have authored almost half of the class's written assignments the last two years. Plus, I use up my choicest words and profoundest ideas when I write Doug's and sweet Lisa's masterpieces. I'm actually relieved each semester when students settle for Bs. I need a couple hours of sleep each night, and an A paper, like the one on page 83, takes me a couple hours or more to write. Writing an A paper's first draft takes longer than writing a B paper's final draft, and then there's all the revision involved in the A paper's second draft, as well. You can't always put a timetable on an A paper, which must demonstrate nimble, original, precise, coherent thinking. You need to walk away from it and then return with fresh eyes and a fresh mind. A two-page B paper, in contrast, always takes me 35–40 minutes. This is why I charge five times more for an A paper. If I didn't charge so much for them, A papers would kill me or my business. Everyone wants one, of course, but I don't have nearly the space in my life to produce more than a few of them each week.

Sometimes, when writing an A paper, you even need to start over. Yep, you heard me right: You may have already chosen a topic or started your paper, but if it's not working for you, you may need to start writing sentences that *are* working for you. Don't believe me? Take this example.

I still remember when, in ninth grade, my English teacher asked us to select a major issue in the news, pick a side, and write a persuasive essay. My geography teacher that year had one of those antiracist posters with pictures of pennants for made-up teams like the Cincinnati Crackers (to illustrate what it must feel like for American Indians to see professional teams named after them, even in derogatory ways), so I decided to argue the other side, defending the Washington Redskins' team name. I thought that trying to come up with such an argument would lead to a passionate, surprising essay. Here's what I came up with (for Doug, believing I was on my way to an A):

> ## What You Don't Know about
> ## the Redskins' Team Name

Yep. That's it. I still don't know how to start this one. Instead, I wrote about tags on the back of T-shirts. They itch, I argued, so shouldn't they go on the *outside* of the shirt instead of on the *inside*? People could come to accept this as cool, and it would be better advertising for the T-shirt brand.

The example A paper I'm going to write next, and for which my buddy Doug will get the credit, will end up on Mr. Spreephy's desk. Mr. Spreephy teaches English to juniors and Humanities to seniors. Seniors take his Humanities course because they're really motivated. At the beginning of the school year, the class gets together off campus, usually at a coffee shop. It often becomes a walking conversation, as they continue to talk during a stroll through the community. With Mr. Spreephy guiding the conversation, they choose twenty books they want to read together that school year. It takes a few hours, of course. Students have strong opinions, and they come prepared to persuade one another, having interviewed their parents and older students, having read book jackets, book reviews, and having researched authors—but there's also compromise. *Okay, you want to read that book? Fine. Can we read this one, too, then?* Before anyone leaves, the twenty books have been selected and placed in reading order based on themes the class has decided to explore. And then, over the course of the school year, they all read those books and talk about them. They often read a full novel in a week. I know all of this not just from hearsay but because I (reluctantly) took the course this year. That's how I know that, in addition to reading each book, they also do some kind of project about each one—a two-page essay or something more creative. This year, we read *Last Days of Summer* by Steve Kluger. It's an epistolary novel, which means it's told in letters back and forth between characters, so during that unit we wrote letters to each other instead of writing essays. Mr. Spreephy's Humanities course is THE great reading and intellectual challenge at our high school, but kids walk away saying it's the best school experience of their lives. They take the class even though they need to take an English class, as well.

I wouldn't have done it, however, if Doug hadn't signed up. When Doug said he wanted to take the class, let's just say I was surprised. No, I was more than surprised. I was angry. That meant I would need to take on a lot of extra work, and I was already stretched thin. Doug said, though, that it would look great on a college transcript. I figured if I was going to have to read all the books so I could write Doug's papers, I might as well get credit for it, so I registered, which means I've been writing more for him this year than ever. In Humanities, we talk about book after book after book. We read newspapers in class and consider how the literature we read relates to what's happening around us. With my business, I'm on a tight deadline all the time, and I don't always have patience for deep learning in class, but even I get swept up in the genuine curiosity that gusts and swirls around Mr. Spreephy's classroom.▼ Doug's the only one I write essays for in Humanities class. I guess if you're going to take this class—put in the time to read those books and fully consider their impact—you don't have any interest in hiring anyone like me.

Mr. Spreephy hands out his final writing assignment with three months left in the school year so we can manage our own time and figure out when to devote the kind of focus we'll need to do it right.:)

▼ Yes, I know how ridiculously idealistic that sounds. But it's true.

:) He's good about this, Mr. Spreephy. We don't all have the same deadline all the time. We don't all turn in the exact same number of papers, either. The only thing he could do to prevent people like me from writing papers for people like Doug? He could have us do a lot of our writing in class instead of out. I don't know why the teachers at my school are so averse to this idea. When we write in class, the teacher's right there to answer questions, and he's all but guaranteed to see our real work. I'm not complaining. If we did this, my business wouldn't exist.

Mr. Spreephy's Annual Spring Writing Prompt/ Book Selection Challenge

Now that you've nearly completed 12th-grade Humanities, you are in a unique position. You've read 20 challenging texts this year by artists such as Toni Morrison, Joseph Heller, Jonathan Kozol, Barbara Kingsolver, Nicole Krauss, Donald Winslow, and Li-Young Lee. You've written about many of these texts, unpacked others through group projects, and discussed all of them in pretty significant depth. It seems you all agree this—the dissection and connection of challenging ideas and stories—is important work. We will have time as a class to reflect on this work, as well as to celebrate it. Now, however, it's time for you to lend me a hand. Every year, as we approach the course's completion, I ask each of my Humanities students to write an essay. Now I'm asking you. In this essay, please propose a summer reading text for next year's Humanities students. Do some thinking about this. You have a whole world of texts to choose from, and I'd like you to pick the one you think will most thoroughly engage next year's class participants as it pushes them to begin playing around with the analysis and communication skills they'll need when school resumes this fall. I will assign the text most convincingly championed by one of you.

I've given myself an entire afternoon to write a draft of this paper for Doug. It's not due until three months from now, either, so I'll have plenty of time to return to and revise my work.

I begin by brainstorming. I start with *The Brothers*

Karamazov by Dostoevsky, because that's what we read last summer. I nearly throttled Doug when I first learned someone had convinced Mr. Spreephy to make us read a 700-page Russian novel. And then, 100 pages into the novel, I was hooked. Aloysha's this guy about my age asking lots of great questions. There's a murder mystery at the center of it all.

I write down novels, plays, and screenplays I've read on my own and for class the last couple years. The novels *Catch-22* by Joseph Heller, *Devil in a Blue Dress* by Walter Mosley, and *The Princess Bride* by William Goldman. The play *Joe Turner's Come and Gone* by August Wilson. The screenplay *Serenity* by Joss Whedon. They'd all give the students a lot to talk about the first week of school. Of course, this needs to be a text students can refer back to throughout the year.

It occurs to me that maybe the book I choose for Doug should be something I know Doug has actually read, just in case Mr. Spreephy selects it and asks my friend questions. I'm not sure Doug has finished a book since middle school, though, besides collections of *Calvin and Hobbes* comics (which, I admit, are always a good choice) and *This Is a Book By Demetri Martin* (also a good choice).

And then it occurs to me, even as a memory from ninth-grade English sprints to the front of my brain. Harry Potter. Doug's read *Harry Potter*. He even liked *Harry Potter*. *Everyone* liked *Harry Potter*, which is why I didn't read the series until more recently, once the peer pressure had died down. While I don't appreciate the cutesy House Cup—you know, "Ten points to Gryffindor!"—most of this story is pretty great. I like the movies, too. There's a lot of smart stuff happening in the Harry Potter series. Plus, a lot of adults would complain that it's just for kids, even though they've read it and gone to all the movies, too, so that gives me someone to argue with.* The idea feels right to me. I take out a new piece of paper and begin writing down everything that comes to mind. Many people call this brainstorming. I, as you know, call it Thought Farting.

The first step toward writing an A essay is to brainstorm on paper. Really. This initial step pays dividends later. I hope you trust me enough by now to believe me. If not, well, I suppose it's your loss. If you don't believe me, it's unlikely you'll ever write A essays. It's even more unlikely you'll make a small fortune writing A essays.

❖ Some of you may have been told never to end a sentence with a preposition, like I just did. I can't tell you how lazy and misinformed this "rule" is. I read somewhere that it came from Western Europe several hundred years ago when people like merchants found ways to make money and so old money families felt threatened. The old money people all got together and said, "We'll make up this secret rule about not ending our sentences with prepositions so we can always identify the phonies, the ones who don't really belong." I have no idea if this story is true, but I allow myself to believe it because whenever anyone tells you there's something you absolutely can't do (besides murder or other stuff that actually hurts people), they're lying. Don't believe them. You always have a choice.

Here's what I write down:

Harry Potter Essay Ideas

- *Recommend Mr. S. assigns entire HP series*
- *Everyone knows the story.*
- *Humanities is all about reading critically—what our stories tell us about our world.*
- *HP insists that its heroes read critically. See talk of Daily Prophet (find page #s later).*
- *In Humanities, we read some "foundational texts" because newer books refer to them. Also to better understand other cultures through their stories. Why not get out ahead of this? Let's read what people will read in 200 years to know more about us.*
- *Yes, it's a lot of reading. Maybe they'll watch the movies instead? Whatever. Students take this class because they want to be challenged. They'll read.*
- *HP always remembers the real (or Muggle) world. Every year in the story, the worlds get closer together. Just like how the big issues in the wizarding world mirror our big issues.*
- *Racism (Mudblood stuff)*
- *Old money (Malfoys and Blacks) vs. new money (reminds me of* The Great Gatsby!)
- *Need examples from texts.*
- *BEGIN WITH ALLIE BOGGS EXAMPLE!*

It takes me twenty minutes to brainstorm in this fashion. That's already half the time it takes me to write a two-page B paper. But this won't be a B paper. This will be an A paper. Yes, A essays require a ton of work and care, but they also give the writer a chance to really think things through and hopefully come up with some ideas other people haven't thought of yet.

I climb the ladder up to my attic bedroom and grab the five Harry Potter books I can find: books 1, 2, 4, 5, and 7 in the series. I'll need these books to look up specific examples that support whatever thesis I end up writing.

I'm not ready to write a thesis, though. I'm ready to write a *lead*—the one that popped into my head as soon as I thought of writing about Harry. Here's another tip: **After brainstorming, always write first what you're most excited to write. The rest will come. This could be your lead, your introduction, something from the middle of the essay, or even your conclusion. Often, you won't even know where it will fit into your essay at first. It doesn't matter. Just write what excites you most. The brainstorming is often just jotting, getting thoughts down as fast as you can. Once you've brainstormed, it's time to start *writing*—one careful sentence and then the next and the next.**

For me, right now, that's the lead. I sit down in front of my laptop, with my notes and the Harry Potter books on the dining-room table, and write this:

The Lead

I remember one—and only one—tenth-grade English class vividly. In the class, we're reading *Romeo and Juliet*, and getting near the end. Friar Lawrence explains his whole Juliet-dead-but-not-*really*-dead plan to her, and one of my classmates blurts what many of us are thinking.

"Wait," he says. "So this potion the friar gives her—it's supposed to make her heart slow down so much she's basically dead for two days and then wakes up? So . . . it kills her but doesn't kill her?"

"That's stupid," says another classmate. "How are we supposed to believe that?"

From a third classmate: "Yeah. How's a potion going to do all of that?"

We all get into it. We pile on. We have our teacher cornered. No, not just our teacher. We have Shakespeare cornered. *We know more than he does*, we think. *Teachers always say he's so smart that we can relate to him 400 years later. But nothing he writes makes any sense, and now we can prove it!*

We complain to each other and stop paying attention to the teacher, confident that we've won this battle. Maybe we won't even need to read the rest of the play.

Mr. Weller, through the victory pandemonium, tries feebly to regain control. "How *are* you supposed to believe that?"

It's that teacher trick—ask a question when you don't know what to say and hope someone will save you. It's not going to work this time, though. We're united, and we're right.

Then we hear Mr. Weller's voice again. "Yes, Allie?"

We look up to see Allie Boggs—the Allie Boggs who always brings some weird but interesting take to every conversation—lowering her arm as she says, "The same way Harry Potter disapparates. Destination, determination, and deliberation. C'mon, people, *Romeo and Juliet's a story*. We need to suspend our disbelief. Not everything needs to actually make sense in *our* world. We need to visit the characters' world; they don't always need to visit ours."

Gulp. The room silences. *You win, Allie. You win, Mr. Weller. You win, Shakespeare. Even you, English class*, we all think, *you win.*

Take note of what I do in the lead here. Does the dialogue pull readers right in? I hope so. It took me thirty minutes to write this lead and another ten to proofread and polish it for the first time. I'll need to return to it later and give it more of my time. Sentences will shift and move. Some will need to be removed. I just don't know which ones yet. I need to return to this lead later with fresh eyes. The lead is worth all of this time, however. In the lead, I get to show readers why this topic matters to me and should matter to them. I want to point something else out, too. See the one-word sentence "Gulp."? If you want to write A papers—or anything that's truly yours and worth a reader's time—then you have to be ready to break a few rules. Like I said earlier, your punctuation should help readers follow your argument and understand your points; so if a sentence without a subject or a predicate (called a fragment by some people, but I just think of it as a different kind of full sentence) helps more than a sentence with both a subject and a predicate, go with it. Even if Microsoft Word puts a squiggly green line under it and calls it a fragment. You—not Microsoft Word—are the author of *your* paper.

Remember my burrito example from earlier? A strong essay is often built like a burrito. A tortilla/introduction provides a surface to build on, you get to add ingredients and change your mind about those ingredients (the claims you flesh out and support throughout the essay) as they most appeal to you, and then you wrap it all up with a tortilla/conclusion which recalls the introduction but now brings everything together while creating something new, something that has grown into a better, more interesting version of what it was when you began. Well, in truth, an A essay's even better than a Chipotle burrito on its own, and that's saying something. The lead to an A essay becomes that story you overheard someone telling a friend about how their parents surprised them with a trip to Chipotle for dinner the previous night. They'd finished soccer practice and hadn't eaten anything since breakfast; they'd never been so hungry, and nothing had ever satisfied them as that Chipotle dinner did. The lead, in other words, whets readers' taste buds. It makes them want to eat that burrito/read that essay. Not that you always have a lead. Every paper's different.

Okay. Knowing I'll go back to this lead later to review and revise, I move to my introductory paragraph.

(How long will this essay be, in the end? I don't know exactly. The best writing doesn't fit into anyone's length requirements. You simply write until you've accomplished your goals as well as goals you didn't know you had. Here, I know Mr. Spreephy will need to read twenty-five essays, so I do him the favor of imagining this essay as no more than a few pages.)

The Introduction

I tell this story now to illustrate why I believe incoming Humanities students should spend the summer reading (or, likely, *re*reading) the Harry Potter series. It's a story everyone's familiar with, but many of us read the books when we were younger, and certainly not for class, and so we give them more leeway than we do the books we read in high school. We allow for parts— characters' decisions, plot movements—to not make complete sense because we have such fond memories of the books and we read them at an age when not everything needed to make literal sense. Rereading them as young adults helps us remember why we read stories in the first place—to be entertained, challenged, and inspired. **Assigning *Harry Potter* sends a message: Students will begin the year reading one of *their* beloved stories critically but without judgment; then they will apply the skills practiced with *Harry Potter* to every other text we read.**

I **bolded** the thesis statement here. Again—not every great essay has a defined thesis, but a lot of them do. As I've said throughout the book, writing is sentence making. I often like to have a thesis statement because it's a part of the essay that honors this concept of each sentence being important and needing to be carefully crafted. Of course, I don't know yet what my conclusion will be, and that's a good thing. I'll have to write until I find what I'm looking for.

I begin typing.

What we learn from *Harry Potter* . . .

I can feel that that sentence will lead to a boring "to be" verb—something like "What we learn from *Harry Potter* **is** that . . ."—and a boring statement. I stop typing.

I begin again.

Rereading *Harry Potter* will . . .

I don't know. I'm just not ready to write this yet. I need to back away from the computer, clear my head, and then let the ideas I brainstormed hunt each other down from opposite sides of my brain and then battle for my attention.

"Banjo!" I call, and I hear my family's Airedale scrape across the library's[⋈] wood floor. He puts his paws on my chest, begins to pee on the floor, and scratches me with his nails as I say, "Wait till we get outside!"

[⋈] Okay, it's not really a library. It's a small bedroom that still belongs to my older brother, though he's out of high school, works at Subway, and has his own efficiency apartment. When he graduated, my parents and I put in these IKEA bookshelves, and that's where we keep most of our books and DVDs.

I manage to get the leash on and then he pulls me out the back door and finishes his peeing on the lawn. By going out the back door, I hope to avoid any other panicked classmates who want to pay me a visit or one with a Quick 16 Blaster aimed at my heart. Banjo and I slip out the back gate, and, immediate urinary needs out of the way, he settles into my walking pace and we head toward the river.

As we walk, I notice the length of each neighbor's grass. Mr. Mickelson's needs to be mowed, like ours, and the Trubbles' lawn looks immaculate as always. I notice these things and the noticing (but not really caring) organizes my mind somehow. My understanding of what I need to do in the essay—even as Banjo squats and does his business and then I bend over and pick it up, my hand inside a plastic bag—becomes clearer.

I'm writing to Mr. Spreephy, and I need to establish that in the beginning. I need to acknowledge him as my (or Doug's) audience.

I need to first address why reading the entire Harry Potter series is necessary and reasonable. The biggest hurdle for incoming students reading these books would be that—devoting enough time to the assignment to finish seven books, books that become substantially longer later in the series.

Banjo stops to sniff yet another tree, tugging me out of my thoughts. "C'mon, boy," I say, and we settle back into a rhythm.

Humanities class demands careful reading, and so does

Harry Potter's story—not just of readers but of its own characters. Yes, that's important.

And why do we read carefully? Stories help us understand each other, right? Help us make sense of other people's decisions and actions.

A block from home, I lean over to pick up another of Banjo's brown presents—my brother calls this process "making bears," probably because in westerns they call urinating "making water," and my brother prides himself on more colorful descriptions—and four yellow darts hit the road behind me. I dive over Banjo and use his big furry body as a shield. "It doesn't count if you hit my dog!" I yell. This doesn't stop Banjo from getting excited when six darts hit him in the head and side. He's ready to play.

"Don't worry about the dog," my stalker says. I try to pinpoint where the voice is coming from while continuing to move away from it. It's all happening too fast again, though, and all I know is this guy's good. "It's not your day, Dremmel." *Doug?* I don't know. Now that I hear the voice again, I'm not even sure it's the same guy who was after me last time. It's a guy's voice again, but this time it's quieter and more menacing?

I twist Banjo's leash around my hand so that it's short, giving me more control, and I pull him sideways, away from where he wants to investigate, keeping him between me and the sniper. I walk backward, still in a crouch, across the street. I see a figure on the other side of the thick, five-foot hedge in my neighbor's yard, but

I can't make out who it is. When I get to the other side of the street, I use the cars parked along the curb as protection, staying low, and Banjo and I scramble home. A couple times, I look through car windows, trying to spot my stalker stepping out from the hedge, but he alludes me.

Banjo and I make it to our property, and I don't dare go through the backyard. To get there, I would first need to get through the fence door, which sticks. Instead, I stay on the other side of the parked cars until I arrive at the front of our house. Then I whisper, "Let's go, boy!" into Banjo's ear and we run like hell across the street. I go in the always unlocked porch door (the porch now providing me with cover), push my key into the lock on the front door, and stumble into the living room of our bungalow house, kicking the door closed behind me.

Banjo bounds through the living room and dining room toward his water dish, pulling me several feet across the wood floor. I dive to grab his collar and finally unclip his leash. I follow him into the kitchen, and hang the leash on a coat hook. I return to the dining room, where my laptop sits on the table with my notes and the five Harry Potter books I found in my bedroom.

I take a deep breath to steady my nerves. The walk-turned-escape has reactivated my mind, and I'm ready to write the rest of the draft. The adrenaline rushing through my body readies me to wrestle with those ideas that wandered into my brain before the darts started flying. Mr. Spreephy, prepare to be persuaded.

The Rest of the Essay:
Sentences that become paragraphs that support and develop the thesis

I predict someone (maybe you, Mr. Spreephy? Or students? Or parents?) might argue that a teacher can't assign this much reading to students over the summer. Over 4,000 pages?! Shouldn't* we leave teenagers with room to read books of their choosing this summer? I understand this argument. I really do. I tend to enjoy books I choose on my own more than assigned books, too. But this course, Humanities, demands that students take on a significant reading challenge throughout the year, and that they embrace the idea of reading

---

❖ *Shouldn't* is a contraction. It brings *Should* and *not* together and represents the missing *o* with an apostrophe. Has anyone ever told you not to use contractions in your papers for school? That, like the rule about never ending a sentence with a preposition or never beginning a sentence with a conjunction, is another one of those made-up rules you don't need to pay attention to. Honestly—it's your job as writer to listen to how the sentence sounds and figure out how it feels. You get to decide what words, in what places, give the sentence better cadence and rhythm. No one ever told you that? Well, it's true. That means you have a responsibility to listen to your own sentences in your head and then make the choices you want to make.

the same books as twenty other students so they can all talk about what they read. There's no better place to start than with rereading the books most of us so loved growing up. *Harry Potter* is the most pervasive and likely enduring tale of our time, and I know most ambitious readers will welcome the (required) opportunity to take lessons at Hogwarts once again. I feel fortunate to live in a moment when my generation has a common text. Nearly everyone has read the series at least once. Absolutely everyone knows the series through exposure to movies and constant allusions in popular culture. Plus, we can all handle the reading: Don't forget that libraries shelve Rowling's books in the *children's* section.

That's not to say, however, that the Harry Potter series doesn't merit close, careful reading. In fact, the series insists that its own main characters read critically and actively. Those with wisdom, for instance, don't trust the Daily Prophet newspaper, which consistently spins and obscures the truth. Hermione tells Harry in *Harry Potter and The Order of the Phoenix*, "But you see what they're doing? They want to turn you into someone no one will believe" (74). Her words resonate. Those who have protested

Harry Potter in our Muggle world worry that the story will corrupt young readers—that it encourages them to believe in witchcraft. But while Hermione says here Harry should be trusted, the author Rowling has a different message: Yes, you should read my work and anything else you can get your hands on—but intelligently, even warily. Harry himself feels fully human, and therefore he has biases and blind spots. Throughout *Order of the Phoenix*, for instance, he is angry and hurt—dealing with pain and confusion and not knowing how—and he lashes out at friends unfairly as a result. Rowling preaches this message of critical reading through her characters from the first book to the last. And in her books, readers will find one particular example that smacks of racism. The goblins who manage the wizarding world's banks evince many of the stereotypes spit at Jewish people through the ages: they're short, "swarthy, clever face[d]" creatures who spend their days "on high stools behind a long counter, scribbling in large ledgers, weighing coins in brass scales, examining precious stones through eyeglasses" (*Sorcerer's Stone* 72–73).

I stop here. I realize that I want to refer to and maybe quote the *Harry Potter* movies, and that means I need to rewatch Harry's first visit to Gringotts Bank. I skate in my socks across the hardwood floors from the dining room table through a short hallway into what we call our library. I go to the DVD bookcase and pull out the boxed set of Harry Potter movies my dad got for my mom and me last Christmas.

I skate back to the living room and place my DVD in the player. I watch the scene, thinking, *Robbie Coltrane makes a great Hagrid*, and then return to my essay.

The popular Harry Potter movie adaptations show the goblins with large, hooked noses; in the film *Harry Potter and the Sorcerer's Stone*, Hagrid says goblins are not "the most friendly of beasts." Near the end of the Harry Potter story, one goblin, Griphook, reinforces these stereotypes when he turns on Harry, Ron, and Hermione in the name of greed and mistrust (*Deathly Hallows* 541). When one reads Rowling's complete work, however, which condemns Nazi Germany through its presentation of the dangerous, manipulative, sycophantic Ministry of Magic, it becomes clear that the goblins do not represent an author's prejudice but that of the context in which she writes her stories. Our context. The context of a world that has recently seen on its walls, even in the previous century, illustrations that stereotyped and caricaturized the Jewish people, connecting exaggerated physical features to types of behavior and personality. The *Harry Potter* movies, after all, present a much more conniving, insatiable goblin race than do Rowling's books. What does this tell us? That Harry Potter's world is still our world, and it's a scary one. A world of prejudice and intolerance. And yet, it's a world of hope, too. Countries do come to the aid of oppressed peoples around the world, and in our literature we cheer for Harry and the people who work together to defeat the tyrant Lord Voldemort. Good wins in the end. *Harry Potter*, like so much of the world's literature, provides a mirror reflecting on the culture from which it came, reflecting on those who tell the tales and on those who listen to them. That's why it's so important that we read often and read carefully. Next year's Humanities students will do well to believe in it. Humanities class reminds students daily of the power accompanying critical reading, and that, above all else, appears to be Rowling's most important point.

Reading voraciously and thoughtfully empowers us to address the big human issues, including racism. In *Harry Potter and the Goblet of Fire*, Hermione, the nonstop reader, begins

S.P.E.W. (The Society for the Promotion of Elfish Welfare). She has the mental agility and compassion to empathize with house-elves who have no rights. She empathizes even with the foulest house-elf in the Harry Potter story, the prejudiced, obscenity-muttering Kreacher, who, by the way, treats Hermione worst of all. In the final book, Hermione explains to Harry, who can't understand Kreacher's motivation for acting as he does, that "Kreacher doesn't think like that. . . . He's loyal to the people who are kind to him" (*Deathly Hallows* 198). She empathizes when others can't because she has spent her life seeing the world from characters' points of view in the books she reads. Ultimately, because Hermione insists on seeing the world from Kreacher's point of view, the house elf begins to adore her, Harry, and Ron. Until this moment, Ron only mocked Hermione for her continued efforts to free elves from what she sees as slavery. "They. Like. It," Ron repeats. "They *like* being enslaved" (*Goblet* 224). And he's right: Many house-elves find comfort in their slavery. The fictional analogy here matches examples we see in history—of certain enslaved Africans and African Americans in America who can't imagine their own freedom clearly enough to dream of it, for instance, or even of prisoners who grow accustomed to their structured life and don't want to leave. Hermione, however, who lives by the creed "When in doubt, go to the library" (*Chamber* 255), sees more in elves than they see in themselves. The best literature does this: It helps us more clearly see the world *we* live in—its people, its questions, its issues—and imagine a better one.

Racism becomes the center-stage issue in the Harry Potter story—that is, wizards treating Muggles (human non-wizards) with disrespect. In addition, old wizarding families such as the Malfoys and Blacks despise wizards who come from Muggle families (called "mudbloods") in much the same way the longtime wealthy in Fitzgerald's *The Great Gatsby* look down on the nouveau riche.◆

In English classes and in Humanities class, we often read texts that belong to some literary canon. Many have stood the test of time, moving from one culture to another to another: *The Odyssey*, *Arabian Nights*, *Beowulf*, *The Canterbury Tales*, and all those Shakespeare plays. We ask what common threads run through these classics. How do they speak to each other? In Humanities class, we read critically, which means figuring out what the stories we read tell us about ourselves and about the

---

◆ At their best, essays often get different texts talking to each other.

people who first read them. In a couple hundred years, I bet people will read *Harry Potter* to find out more about how people thought and lived in the twentieth and twenty-first centuries.

Perhaps most important, *Harry Potter* reminds us of what Allie Boggs said: We need to spend more time visiting characters' worlds than they do ours. When we visit characters' worlds—when we walk in their shoes, as Harper Lee put it—we begin to appreciate, or at least understand, their points of view. That's called empathy, and developing empathy is why we read stories in the first place. We were capable as children of reading challenging texts and empathizing with characters who live in different worlds. High school seniors should reread *Harry Potter* to be reminded that they're still capable of empathetic reading, no matter how strange the characters and their decisions feel at first.

And there it is—a draft of an A paper. If you glance back at the paragraphs, you'll notice that each one has a topic sentence (that is, the first sentence of the paragraph says something hopefully interesting) and builds to a concluding sentence. This is something I now do instinctively, unless I intentionally choose to create some other kind of paragraph, such as a one-sentence paragraph, because I like the sound of it or I want to emphasize the words.

Like this.

You paid more attention to those words because I gave them their own paragraph, right?

After glancing over my essay, knowing I'll reread it more carefully later, I go back to the beginning and add a title to the essay that occurs to me now: "Choose *Harry Potter* or I'll Jinx You, Muggle."

* * * * *

Tonight, Friday night, I lie back on my bed, exhausted. That Harry Potter essay took a lot out of me, and then I wrote two C-plus and three B-plus essays before calling it quits for the night.

Is it worth it? I ask myself, as I do many nights, when my brain feels scrambled and numb at the same time from all the writing.

I get up and move to my desk, where I have one of those calculators your grandparents use with the big buttons. I could find my exact profit online at my bank's website, or I could do the simpler, rounded math in my head, but there's something satisfying in watching the numbers grow on the calculator's screen. I don't need to know the number to the penny right now; I just need reassurance that my business efforts have paid off.

I punch 45 into the calculator. It's a ballpark, conservative number. I began with thirty-three clients and

now have seventy-four (with seven new customers sign-
ing contracts before senior year). I haven't worked with
all of them for the last three and a half years, though,
so I pick a number between the two and closer to the
original thirty-three.

Most of my clients pay for Bs, which cost $20 apiece,
so I hit the multiplication button and then twenty.
That's $900 for one paper per client. I write about
twenty papers a year for each customer, which means
$18,000 a year. I round down and tell the calculator
I've been at this for 3.5 years, and there it is—a pretty
close estimate of what I've earned as a high school essay
writer: $63,000.

Yeah, okay. So it's worth it.

There's a knock on my door, which is a rectangle in
the floor a few feet from my bed.

"Who is it?" I say. My voice has a scruffy quality.
I'm not sure it's even mine. It's been a while since I
spoke to another person.

My mom's voice: "The phone's for you, Charles."

Great. I don't answer my cell phone so someone
calls my home phone.

I go to the door in the floor, pull it up, and my mom,
standing halfway up the ladder below the hatch, hands
me the phone. "You look tired, Charles," she says. "Get
some sleep."

I nod and drop the rectangle of wood back in place.

"Yeah," I say into the phone, my voice now scruffy
and angry. No answer. "Hello?"

"Oh—sorry," a voice on the other end says to me. "I didn't know you were talking to me. This is Sidney."

I'm dazed and don't follow right away.

"Sidney Little?" the voice explains. "From English class?"

"Oh, Sid. Hey," I manage. "Why didn't you call my cell phone?"

"Sorry—couldn't find the number. Guess what? I just used a phone book. A phone book! Can you believe it? I had to ask my parents if I should use the yellow one or the white one. Anyway, I was thinking about what you said—you know, grandparents liking Bs and all. I signed up for extra shifts today at Terry's. I'll miss a few classes, but I can pay for higher grades on my papers now."

I smile. I'm still tired, but the business deal rejuvenates me some. This will mean more work for me. It will also mean more money. "You got it, Sid. Swing by tomorrow before school and we'll revise the contract."

The Next Several Weeks

Life, as it so often does, falls into a pattern. I get up, shower, eat breakfast, and sprint to school, which means I sit in my own sweat during first period, until it has time to dry as my body cools down. I don't want to ride with Doug because he might want to shoot me. Yes, a part of me—okay, a very large part—still cares about the Nerf War. There's just not anything I can do without knowing the name of my next target, and Marc Pride—when I bug him about it—maintains he has no idea where his index card went. I avoid Doug and his car with the Quick 16 Blaster above the backseat.

My customers grow more and more worried. I swear I see nervous ticks and bulging veins. Chris Rinkles always wears a layer of cool over his anxiety, but I can see that this is really weighing on him. He, like most customers, has resigned to the fact that he won't know anything more until I tell him, and he leaves me alone. I send out reassuring text messages every now and then, like this:☼

> Every episode of Full House ends
> with hugs. So will your senior year.
> I really do have a plan.

Or this:

> Which is truer? Patience is
> a virtue. Charles Remington
> Dremmel is a genius. No matter
> your answer, you should feel
> confident.

Or this:

> Roses are red, violets are violet.
> Not only is this version more pre-
> cise but it also reinforces that you
> don't need to think about that
> other color at all.

Life grows monotonous and, I admit, lonely.♥

☼ What? You don't know the show *Full House*? You should. It's the best bad TV show ever. YouTube it. Yep, that's John Stamos with the mullet. Nope, that's not Elizabeth Olsen; it's her twin sisters, Mary Kate and Ashley.

♥ Some of you (very few, I'm sure) will want an update on the Lisa Kent situation. Unfortunately, there's no situation, as there never will be, outside of me writing her papers and her writing "You make me laugh. I hope we have a class together next year." in my yearbook. Well, not even that anymore. I mean, we're graduating from high school. I never see her, anyway, because she's always rehearsing for that *Hamlet* show. I would go to the play, even if Lisa's not playing Jasmine, but teachers can't help themselves from assigning my customers more and more work as we the end of the school year comes into view.

Monday, May 24

Nearly three months later, I send this text message to all of my customers:

> Meet me at Star View Drive-In
> tonight. 1:00 a.m. No excuses. Be
> there. Your future in education
> depends on it.

I'm not sure that's what they teach in customer relations classes—that 1:00 a.m. is the best time to do business—but it will have to do.

I knock on the door to the Star View's projector room at 12:27, and Doug is already there. I look around the room for Doug's Quick 16 Blaster, because I still can't be sure he's not the one after me. But I'm tired, and I'm glad to see him, and I realize if anybody's going to shoot me I hope it's him.

"Thanks for meeting me," I say.

"Of course, Chuckles." He rubs his eyes and sits down in a rolling chair. "Kinda late, huh?"

"It's the only time I knew no one would have conflicts—"

"Besides sleep," Doug interrupts. "Some might plan to sleep in the middle of the night."

I continue: "And it's the only time I thought we could avoid adults for an hour."

Doug shrugs. "So why here, at the Drive-In? You got a movie to show?"

"Something like that," I say. I pluck the flash drive from my pocket and walk over to the computer from which Doug's parents play their second-run movies. "Hey—can I hide out back here until one? I don't want to have to explain myself to them more than once."

Doug shrugs again. "No problem." He leans back in his chair and closes his eyes.

Over the next twenty-six minutes, as I sit hidden in the dark on the projector room's floor, my customers arrive. "Where's Dremmel?" they say. "He better have a real plan." I hear fear in some of their voices. Anger in others. Irritation in all of them.

At precisely 1:00, I step out of the projector room.

 According to my cell phone, which gets its time from a satellite. Apparently, in some way I don't really understand, people around the world set their watches to London's Big Ben. If that's true, the world trusts an old clock (or a cracked bell inside that old clock). Which doesn't sound very sensible until I remember that I've insisted my customers trust me for months, and I'm just one person like Big Ben is one clock (or bell). Maybe my customers should call me Big Charles from now on. I have no idea why I just shared this with you. Give me a break. It's one in the morning.

As soon as I do, someone shouts, "There he is!" And then it starts:

"Hey—Dremmel! Why are we here?"

"Please tell me you have a plan."

"I've been bugging him for months, and he picks now—now—one in the morning—to finally talk?"

I'm not sure how to get them to stop talking to me and to each other. I don't like to shout, and I'm not sure shouting would work anyway.

That's when I find myself doing something unplanned. I'm raising my hand—that gesture all of my middle-school teachers used to get our attention.

Somehow, it works. My classmates raise their hands, too, and stop talking. They must be as shocked by the gesture as I am.

"Right," I say. "Okay. So first—presents."

My dad's car—a fifteen-year-old navy blue Toyota Corolla rusted around the wheels—is parked right up front. I turn my back to my audience, pop the trunk, and reveal its treasure: manila folders with classmates' names on them. There are folders in the back seat, too. Customers who've been with me for multiple years have three or four folders each.

"These folders," I announce, turning around again, "contain every paper I've written for you, plus all of the Thought Farts you've ever given me.

"When I call your name, please come get your folders."

So this is what we do.

Classmates ask, "What do I need these for?" and I ignore them, something at which I've become awfully adept.

In seventeen minutes—again, according to my cell phone—I'm in front of the group again, raising my hand. This time, I don't get away with it.

"Yeah, we get it. You want our attention," says Max Latterly, who's wearing, as always, his Soc letterman jacket. "But we're not twelve." I don't remember Max listening all that well when he was twelve, but he has a point.

"Fair enough," I say. "So—I bet you're wondering why I gave these back to you."

"You bet? We all just asked you that," someone replies.

I continue. This part, I've rehearsed: "And I bet you're wondering what's going to happen with your Blue Book exams next week."

Someone laughs. "Yeah. He's a genius all right. I've really been paying this guy to write my papers?"

I forge ahead, undeterred: "Well"—[dramatic pause]—"that's up to you. You are going to write your own Blue Book exams."

A lot of shouting and swearing and threatening follows. Then Chris Rinkles shouts, "Shut up, everyone!" They do.

He turns to me and says, "So then, Charles, what do I pay you for then? And what about the contract? You always said I'd get caught if I started writing my own papers again." Even Chris, who's a decent, patient guy, adds some colorful language as he asks his question.

I look at him and then at the rest of them. "In this case, Chris, you're paying me to teach you. Doug," I call back to the projector room, "will you please turn on the projector?"

He does, and an image appears on the massive screen behind me. That image gets brighter and brighter as the projector heats up.

Soon, they can all see it: a schedule, with their names—all of them—on it, divided into groups based on the essay grades they pay for.

"I'm going to meet with you every day from now until you take your Blue Book exams. Each grade group gets an hour and fifteen minutes of my time each day. We'll meet at my house. We'll break down your writing habits—well, the ones I've given you—so you know them and can reproduce them as well as I can. Your first homework assignment will be rereading all of your papers* before your meeting with me tomorrow. Please come with a list of at least five things you notice your teachers writing over and over."

Hal Burk, whose been studying the projected

---

* Why don't more people reread their own papers? I can't tell you how many people I've heard say, "I didn't even read it before I handed it in. I just finished and printed." That's before they hire me, of course, as I make customers read the papers with their names on them. But really— why would someone else want to read something even you don't want to look at? That's why your most important job as writer is writing the paper *you* want to read. Establish a rule for yourself: NBP (No Boring Papers). Unless, of course, you're hired to write boring papers.

schedule closely, says, "What about me? I don't see my name up there."

And there it is, another business opportunity.

"Hal, you and the others who pay for Ds don't need my help. Just show up next week and write the exam without taking it too seriously. But if you want to pay for a C, you're welcome to join that group."

He laughs at the idea. Then his tone gets serious. "So why am I here at one thirty in the morning?"

"So I could explain this to everyone at once." When he rolls his eyes, I realize he's right. It would have been a nice gesture if I'd let the D students know my plan at a different time. Still, this week, I'll be busy, every moment that I'm not sleeping or in class, helping class-mates notice their own writing (or what I wrote, posing as them).

Tuesday, May 25, Wednesday, May 26, et cetera

I spend the week with my customers. I never really get used to seeing people so often. Years of essay-writing seclusion have trained me to be more comfortable alone.

From 3:15 to 4:30, I work with the C writers. We meet in the living room and dining room (one room, really, with an arch between the spaces). Every session, I ask my customers to take out their new lists of at least five things they noticed teachers writing more than once in their essays. I give them a prompt, something to write about (for example, "Write about a time when you weren't sure what do to"), and tell them to make all the mistakes their teachers have been pointing out as they respond to that prompt. If you're reading this and you no longer want to start a business but you do want to write better essays, you should look through past papers and do what my customers are doing now—except instead of mimicking previous blunders, you should learn from them as you write stronger sentences. As my customers write, I move around the room and talk one-on-one with each customer about what she saw while looking through each paper and the steps she's taking to replicate "her" writing style.

From 4:45 to 6:00, I work with the B writers. We follow the C writers' steps from earlier this afternoon. Of course the B writers notice different stuff. (See my earlier commentary on what a C essay looks like and on what a B essay looks like.)

And from 6:00 until 11:00 or so, I work with the A writers. My parents are home by now,✧ so we move to my bedroom in the attic. This work demands much more time because writing an A essay takes longer and because I'm training six people—including my best friend, Doug, and the love of my life, Lisa Kent— who haven't written their own essays in years to now write masterpieces. I know we won't get there, but I do hope we can get close enough that, on an in-class writing exam, they each produce something kraptaculous enough that their work doesn't alarm their teachers, raise suspicions, lead to all of us getting in trouble. These sessions are the most fun. I take them through "their" previous A essays and demonstrate my process. Each night, we break intermittently, and I insist that they each take walks to clear their heads.

✧ They, my parents, couldn't be more pleased, as they watch my classmates shuffle out of the house. They used to express their worry daily that I didn't have very many friends, and now look! I'm so popular I could be homecoming king.

By the way—no, I never forget that Lisa Kent is in my bedroom.

During one of our breaks, as I hand Doug Banjo's leash, he says, "You sure you're not doing this so you don't have to pick up after your dog?" On Wednesday, he jogs to the park with a basketball and shoots hoops instead.

That first night, Tuesday, Lisa says, "Wanna walk with me? It's getting kind of dark."

Of course I want to. But that's not what I say. "This . . . uh . . . it needs to be alone time, Lisa. Where you can gather your thoughts, you know?"

Don't judge me. There's truth to that. And really, what are we going to talk about? We've already been talking about essay writing all night, and we're not gonna talk Nerf War because I don't want her to think I'm any more of a dork than she already does.

Lisa, Doug, and the other A writers do a ton of writing this week. They brainstorm and then they write some more. They read short essays by Neil Gaiman, Philip Pullman, Sherman Alexie, and others between sessions, and then come prepared to talk about voice.

This schedule persists over the weekend. Saturday looks the same as the rest of the week. On Sunday, there's no more teaching. Instead, I give my customers a prompt on the books they're reading in English: *Of Mice and Men* by Steinbeck in the regular track, *Grendel* by Gardner in the honors track. They get the same hour to write it on Sunday as they will the next day, which will be a different prompt, I'm sure. Each customer has made real progress in emulating the writing style I created for them. Even Max Latterly. I'm impressed, if not surprised, by how much a writer can improve when he begins to notice and care.

I work longer with Lisa and Doug and the other A writers. We read some more essays. They write several introductions in response to their *Grendel* prompt before each choosing one and then writing an essay, keeping extra paper with them so they can scribble ideas when they have them and then fit them into the essay when the moment arrives.

Now, we hope for the best.

It's Lisa's idea that we should all go get a late dinner together. "Perkins won't be too busy," she says. Doug says he's in, two of the others agree, and of course I do, too. If Doug will be there, I'll have conversational protection.

We agree to all go home (easy for me), shower, change, push essay writing from our minds, and reconvene here.

In the shower, I consider what this essay-writing business has gotten me. The results aren't necessarily pretty. On the drawbacks side of the T-chart: few friends, no social life to speak of, a life of little spontaneity or free time. I admit, I'll be happy when it's over. On the benefits side of the T-chart: money, which means a chance to go to college. Really, that's it, unless you count tonight: one dinner with a pretty girl, and not only my best friend but two other classmates will be there. So it's not like I'm going to dinner with a pretty girl.

I join my parents on the couch as they watch the nine o'clock news. Mom says what she always says: "Charles, you look exhausted."

My dad says, "It's been fun to meet all of your friends, if ever so briefly."

"They're not my friends, Dad."

My parents both look confused. To make them, but not me, feel better, I add, "But I am going out to dinner tonight with some of them."

It works. They smile.

The doorbell rings, and I go to get it. I walk out the front door to the porch and see Lisa Kent, hands behind her back, beautiful brown eyes meeting mine through the porch's screen door. I open the door and am about to stammer, "Hey, Lisa," when she pulls from behind her back a Quick 16 Blaster and pumps all 16 darts into my chest.

"You, my friend," says Lisa, "are officially eliminated. I can't believe how hard it's been to finish this job. Can I drop the gun here while we go to dinner?"

She has a wide smile on her face.

At dinner, she explains how she followed me out to the copse of trees that day. How she bought Marc Pride's index card from him. How she almost got me that day

I walked Banjo. How with *Hamlet* rehearsal she hasn't had a chance to catch me alone again, especially since I wouldn't walk with her this week. How she played a split-personality Rosencrantz and Guildenstern and had to invent two guys' voices to pull off the part. All of this means she's been stalking me, and so I smile all the way through my Perkins bread-bowl salad.

I told you earlier that an essay is like a burrito or a pitcher in baseball or a stand-up comedian's story or an unexpected thank-you card or an overheard conversation. I stand by those similes. But now I have a better one.

An essay is like a Nerf War. That makes it a joke you take seriously because, even if you can't explain it, it matters to you.

It demands focus. It requires you to plan and prepare but also to act on instinct at times and exercise flexibility as you respond to emerging situations (or ideas, in an essay). And when you get to the end, you're often surprised to have found something even better than what you originally planned, because you learned along the way.

My legacy: Sixteen darts in the chest courtesy of my new favorite assassin and one week in which I forced my classmates to care about their writing. And that's enough. Well, that and the execution of a business that will pay my college tuition.[:)]

[:)] If, of course, I don't get caught and banished from academia for life.

Appendix

Verbs I Used in This Document That You Might Consider Using in Your Writing, Too

allow
appear
applaud
approach
arrive
assume
bear
bellows
block
bother
bound
charge
clutter
compel
complain
convince
cope
corner
correspond

corrupt
dance
dart
devote
disapparate
discourage
disregard
drive
dry heave
feature
fend
flip
follow
forge
gust
hook
illustrate
interchange
jar

jinx

jump-start

mumble

muster

nudge

obscure

pancake block

perspire

plug

polish

pump

rejoice

remain

remember

remonstrate

remove

resonate

respond

riddle

ring up

roar

rush

separate

shift

shove

skate

skip

slip

snake

sniff

squat

stretch

suspect

swamp

swim

swing

swirl

switch

tackle

unclip

watch

whisper

Acknowledgments

I owe recognition to more people than I can efficiently thank here at the end of this book. The list includes my teachers, from grade school through graduate school, who relished books with me and encouraged my writing. It includes the students at St. Paul Academy and Summit School, with whom I'm grateful to share a classroom five days a week. This, of course, is a diverse group: some tall, some short; some reserved, some outspoken; all of them interesting; all of them with thoughts and stories and words worthy of my attention and yours. Their work, their curiosity, their reading proclivities, their senses of humor—these certainly helped shape my book. I wrote it for them and young writers like them. One student, Daniela Tiedemann, deserves my gratitude above all others. Her skillful, creative illustrations help the world (or at least, hopefully, a few readers) *see* my corny punctuation metaphors. The list of those I need to thank also includes my teaching colleagues. Every day I collaborate with and learn from people who care about kids and want what's best for them, and I know how lucky I am to do so.

Barbara Swanson, Michele Dunn, my talented brother, Patrick, and the incomparable Carrie Clark read early drafts of this book and provided crucial feedback and support.

I need to thank, also, William Strunk, Jr., and E. B. White, Lynne Truss, Stephen King, Mike Reynolds, Stanley Fish, Karen Elizabeth Gordon, Verlyn Klinkenborg, and Nancie Atwell. Their books and perspectives on writing and teaching writing inform my book and my life's work. Through their contributions I gained a sense of what was already out there for writers and what wasn't.

Thank you to Cedar Fort, and in particular to Jennifer Fielding. Thrice you've helped me bring my story to a broader audience. I'm grateful also for Melissa Caldwell's careful editing.

I feel the need to say thanks a second time to my brother, Patrick, also a writer and teacher, and always my first and smartest reader. He gets this paragraph all to himself.

At the end of every book, and at the beginning, and in the middle, for that matter, I know the ultimate thanks goes to my wife, Debbie. Teaching and writing demand a great deal of time, and I have a spouse—busy and ambitious in her own right—who supports my long hours and doesn't even roll her eyes too often when she sees me reading books—full books!—about syntax or punctuation. I owe you several games of Ms. Pac-Man, Dizz.

Works Cited

Fitzgerald, F. Scott. *The Great Gatsby.* New York: Scribner, 2004.

Harry Potter and the Sorcerer's Stone. Dir. Chris Columbus. Warner Bros., 2001. DVD.

Hinton, S. E. *The Outsiders.* New York: Penguin, 1967.

Rowling, J. K. *Harry Potter and the Sorcerer's Stone.* New York: Scholastic, 1997.

———. *Harry Potter and the Chamber of Secrets.* New York: Scholastic, 1999.

———. *Harry Potter and the Goblet of Fire.* New York: Scholastic, 2000.

———. *Harry Potter and the Order of the Phoenix.* New York: Scholastic, 2003.

———. *Harry Potter and the Deathly Hallows.* New York: Scholastic, 2007.

About the Author

Andy Hueller is the author of *Dizzy Fantastic and Her Flying Bicycle* and *Skipping Stones at the Center of the Earth*. He teaches at St. Paul Academy and Summit School and lives in Minneapolis with his wife, Debbie. Learn more about Andy, "Charles," Cal, and of course Dizzy at andrewhueller.com. And pick up helpful writing tips from "Charles" at grammarmagic.blogspot.com.